Tennis Shoes

OTHER YEARLING BOOKS YOU WILL ENJOY:

MOVIE SHOES, *Noel Streatfeild*
TRAVELING SHOES, *Noel Streatfeild*
SKATING SHOES, *Noel Streatfeild*
THEATRE SHOES, *Noel Streatfeild*
DANCING SHOES, *Noel Streatfeild*
BALLET SHOES, *Noel Streatfeild*
THE SECRET GARDEN, *Frances Hodgson Burnett*
A LITTLE PRINCESS, *Frances Hodgson Burnett*
HARRIET THE SPY, *Louise Fitzhugh*
THE LONG SECRET, *Louise Fitzhugh*

YEARLING BOOKS are designed especially to entertain and enlighten young people. Charles F. Reasoner, Professor Emeritus of Children's Literature and Reading, New York University, is consultant to this series.

For a complete listing of all Yearling titles, write to Dell Publishing Co., Inc., Promotion Department, P.O. Box 3000, Pine Brook, N.J. 07058.

Tennis Shoes

Noel Streatfeild

A YEARLING BOOK

Published by
Dell Publishing Co., Inc.
1 Dag Hammarskjold Plaza
New York, New York 10017

Copyright © 1956 by Noel Streatfeild

All rights reserved. No part of this book may be reproduced
or transmitted in any form or by any means, electronic or
mechanical, including photocopying, recording, or by any
information storage and retrieval system, without the written
permission of the Publisher, except where permitted by law.

Yearling ® TM 913705, Dell Publishing Co., Inc.

ISBN: 0-440-48605-X

RL: 4.7

Printed in the United States of America

December 1984

10 9 8 7 6 5 4 3 2

CW

Contents

1

How They Got the Tennis House

The Heaths lived at Tulse Hill. Their father was a doctor. He had not meant to be a doctor. He would have liked to be a soldier; but in an accident he was shot through the leg. Unfortunately his leg was very badly hurt and he walked lame ever afterward. Obviously soldiers have to have both their legs working properly, so he became a doctor instead. He was not the rich sort of doctor people go to see in Harley Street, paying five guineas a visit; but the sort that looks after large families. Dr. Heath quite understood about large families, having four children of his own.

Mrs. Heath was just the right sort of wife for a doctor. She always remembered what had been the matter with the patients, and asked after them when she met them outside, and sent around flowers, and lent books when they were ill, and sometimes, when they were convalescent and had no garden, suggested they would get well quicker if they came and sat in hers. She had been very pretty when Dr. Heath married her, but being busy and running in and out in all weather had made her skin rather rough, and anxious times over money had turned some of her hair gray. It did not matter about these things, because neither Dr. Heath nor the children would have anything about her different; they all thought her perfect as she was.

The four Heath children were called Jim, Susan, Nicolette, and David. Jim and Susan were twins. All the children had different shades of red hair. They got this from their father and their grandfather, who were red-headed. Grandfather was not red anymore except in one little patch in his left eyebrow. Jim's hair was really just barely red; many people would have called it sandy. Susan was the beauty of the family. Her hair was the lovely shade of red; it was long, and it curled. At parties and things like that it was combed out and worn loose, and people admired it, which she hated because she was shy. Ordinary days she wore it in two braids. She was rather tall for her age and thin, and had reddish-brown eyes and a pink-and-white complexion. Nicolette, who was always called Nicky because Nicolette really is a mouthful when you are speaking in a hurry, had not nearly as nice hair as Susan's. It was a very orange-red and it was straight. She wore it short, with bangs. As soon as she was old enough to notice people at all she wished she looked like Susan. It seemed hardly fair that Susan should have both things, prettiness and curls. Prettiness she could have done without at a pinch, but she did grudge the curls. Curls are so easy to keep tidy. David had the sort of hair which made it absolutely certain that wherever he went in life he would be called Ginger. Sometimes he was called Rogers after the film star. This sounded like a compliment but it was not meant as one, and he never thought it was. From the time he could speak at all well he had a passion for long words. He would spend hours looking them up in a dictionary. Sometimes he used the words in the right places, but not always.

Annie was the cook-general. Once, soon after Dr. and Mrs. Heath were married, a traveling circus left an acrobat behind in a hospital. She was the daughter of a trapeze artist. She had spent almost all her life in pink tights, jumping off into the air from one trapeze, catching her father by the ankles as she went, turning a somersault, and landing on another trapeze. Then one day, when she was twenty-one, she missed her father's ankles, fell into the net at an awkward angle, and broke her left arm in about eight places. Dr. Heath was one of the people who helped put it together again. He got fond of Annie while this was happening, and so he was the person chosen to tell her that her arm would always be stiff, she could never be a trapeze artist anymore. Annie had stared at him in horror.

"Then what will I do, sir? I couldn't fancy a shooting gallery at a fair or anything like that. Dad won't want me traveling along with him if I can't work in the act."

"Well, can you cook?" Dr. Heath asked her.

"Cook!" She put an immense amount of expression into the word. "If you had lived in a trailer and had to cook for eight on a small stove, you would say you could cook."

"Well, then," he suggested, "we have no cook. How about you coming to us?"

So Annie came to the house on Tulse Hill. She was rather a rough-and-ready cook and never got away from a fondness for suggesting "How about a bit of tripe and onions?" People in the circus had liked tripe and onions. On the other hand, people in the circus had raged at her if they thought the food bad; so it was very easy to tell her something not very complimentary without hurting her feelings. This is not a usual feature in cooks and Mrs. Heath found it very endearing.

Annie never quite gave up thinking of herself as a trapeze artist. She generally announced the meals were ready by saying:

11

"Whoop, whoop, coming over."

There was one other person in the Heath household and that was Miss Pinn. Lucy Pinn had been trained to be a governess. While she was still training, but before she had ever had a situation, her mother, who was a widow, got ill and asked her to come home. For eleven years she stayed at home nursing her mother. In the end her mother died, but not before what money there was had been spent trying to get her well. It was not a very cheerful state of affairs for Lucy Pinn. No money, no work, and not a very good chance of getting work because as she had never had a situation she had never had a reference, and people are very tiresome about wanting references. Dr. Heath had looked after Mrs. Pinn and during the eleven years, he had come to have a great respect for Lucy. It happened that when Mrs. Pinn died the house at Tulse Hill was desperately in need of someone else to look after it besides Annie, and he saw that here was a lovely way out for everybody. Miss Pinn should live with them, teach the children, and do anything else that turned up.

As a matter of fact, in the end she did no teaching at all. When the twins were eight, Susan was sent to St. Clair's College and Jim to a preparatory school at Eastbourne. Susan was so happy at St. Clair's that Nicky was sent to the kindergarten there before she was seven. David was only four at this time, so he did not need much teaching. The result was that Miss Pinn spent all her time doing "anything else that turned up." She did everything about the house that Annie did not do, which really was almost everything except the cooking. Sometimes, when Annie had what she called one of her "sick 'eadicks," which she said made her feel as though she were swinging on a trapeze upside down with her stomach in her mouth,

12

she did the cooking too. She spent all her spare time sewing. She looked very odd herself, for she considered that she was not worth dressing. Her skirts were generally longer behind than in front, and she usually had under one ear a bow that was meant to be under her chin. This lack of interest in her own clothes seemed to make her fonder of other people's. She spent hours poring over paper patterns in *Weldon's* and *Harper's Bazaar* or copying designs out of *Vogue,* in order that Susan and Nicolette should look smart. The only hours that she was smart herself were when she was letting in the patients. For this she wore a white coat which covered her up all over and made her look as though she were a nurse. By the time she had been in the house at Tulse Hill a month, she had dropped being Miss Pinn and was just Pinny to everybody, except Annie, who called her "that Miss Pinn."

The house at Tulse Hill was long and thin and Victorian. It had a porch and a flight of steps leading to the front gate. Annie said she would rather spend her days being the back end of a horse in the circus ring than clean those steps, but she did clean them every morning just the same. When Dr. and Mrs. Heath had first gone to live in the house Mrs. Heath had been in despair over it.

"Oh, Edward!" she said, for that was Dr. Heath's name. "It's much too big for us. Three floors, and all that garden to keep up."

Of course the house stopped feeling too big when the four children arrived, but it was always a difficult house to keep in order when there was not a great deal of money to spend. It seemed to need such a lot of carpet and so many curtains. Of course, carpets and curtains being expensive, the same ones went on year after year, except when they were taken up, or taken down, to be cleaned each spring. But they were a constant anxiety,

13

and both Pinny and Mrs. Heath spent a lot of time on their knees darning holes, and a lot of time with their arms above their heads mending frayed borders.

When the twins were quite tiny Mrs. Heath had looked after them herself and tried to do everything else as well, except the cooking and letting in the patients, which she left to Annie. This had worked fairly well until Nicky arrived. When she was born the twins were two and a bit, and it was almost impossible to keep an eye on them, wash and dress a baby, and do the work of a big house. Of course it ended in disaster. Jim got through the little gate at the top of the stairs and rolled down to the bottom and cut his head open and had to have four stitches put in. Annie got so confused with trying to help as well as do the cooking and the patients, that she went to the front door with a big bit of dough in her hand, which she left stuck on the door handle. The dough came off on a rather grand patient as she was going out, and she was cross and went to another doctor. Nicky was left lying in her cot so long by herself that she got bored, rolled over, and stuck a safety pin into her behind, which hurt so she cried until she almost had convulsions. In fact, the house was in a shocking muddle. Dr. Heath said they must have more help, and more help they had. They had Flossie, Maud, Elsie, Sybil, Doris, and a handyboy called Fred. None of them stayed more than a few weeks, for none of them could get on with Annie. Annie said they were a poor lot of trash who didn't know a trapeze act from a conjuring trick. She said she was not having suchlike in the "big top," which was what she called her kitchen. It was no good Mrs. Heath's pointing out that a servant did not really need to know how to turn somersaults in the air, and whatever she called it, the kitchen was only a kitchen and not a circus tent, for Annie's only answer was: "It's them or me." Even if Pinny had been one half as nice as she was, she could not have failed to have been a success, for when she came to the house it settled down.

The children were rather bright as a family. Susan was clever at lessons. She was always working with girls at least a year older than herself. Jim was good at swimming. Nicky was not outstanding, she was only ordinarily intelligent, and she was lazy; she was generally about the oldest in her class at school and not at the top of it. David had a really good singing voice. They were all a bit ashamed of this in David, because he had to sing songs like *Cherry Ripe* at concerts in aid of charities and churches. He was always encored and was cocky for days afterward. The others thought it would be a very good thing when his voice broke. There was one thing they were all good at, and that was tennis.

The children's grandfather, their father's father, had been first-class at tennis. In his day it had been an odd thing to be first-class at. Most people played pat-ball and were not ashamed of it. Their father had been good, too, but of course his leg injury put an end to his playing. It was when Susan and Jim were nine, Nicky nearly seven, and David four, that tennis first became important in their lives. They were staying with their grandfather. Pinny had taken them down to play in the garden. Their father had given the twins rackets for their last birthday, and they were on the tennis court playing a match of a sort. While they were in the middle of it their grandfather, father, and mother came out and sat and watched the game. Grandfather saw Jim serve a ball and Susan return it, and he stiffened like an old war-horse who smells gunpowder after many years.

"Edward, there's style about those two. What are you going to do about it?"

15

Dr. Heath nodded.

"I know. I've been watching them. Might put up a board in the garden at home and give them a bit of practice."

Grandfather grunted.

"That's a bit like learning to swim a hundred miles from the sea. Couldn't they join a club where they can practice all the year round?"

Mrs. Heath made a face at her husband behind Grandfather's back. The face was meant to say "Agree with him, but of course we can't afford it." Grandfather said he was a little shortsighted but he never missed things like faces made behind his back.

"Now, then, Mollie, I know what that face means. But where there's a will there's a way."

The match between Jim and Susan came to an end. Jim had won. Susan had been winning, but her game had gone right off the moment she realized the grown-ups were watching. Grandfather got up and waved his stick at Pinny.

"Hi! Put Nicky and David on the court. I'm coming down to serve a few balls at 'em. He turned around and he winked at his son, as much as to say: "Trust the old man to see if they're going to be any good."

Neither Nicky nor David had played much. There was a court only when they were staying with Grandfather and the only rackets were the ones that belonged to the twins, and they were not often allowed to borrow them. They were enchanted to play a game with Grandfather. Of course, it was not a bit like tennis. Balls going all over the place and not very often over the net, but Grandfather seemed pleased, and only stopped serving to them because Pinny said that schoolroom tea was ready.

16

When the children had gone in Grandfather came back to his chair.

"Let 'em have a chance." He raised his left eyebrow and the sun glinted on his little cluster of red hairs. "I know it costs money, and things are a bit tight. But it's wonderful how you can save a bit. What you need is a moneybox." He nudged his daughter-in-law. "That's true, eh, Mollie? Now what I shall do is to drive into Salisbury tomorrow. I saw something at old Burns the goldsmith's the other day. Just the thing. I'll be off and get it."

He was good as his word. The next morning there was the most tremendous bustle. Grandfather usually did not come down until about eleven, because of his heart being weak. This morning, however, he was standing in the hall at half-past ten with James, his manservant. James had a plaid rug over his arm. Grandfather never used an automobile. Hibbert, the coachman, had been coachman to his father. He could never learn to drive a car, as he was a very old man. Besides, he would never have tried, for he loved horses. "Horses are good enough for me until old Hibbert goes," Grandfather always said; and Hibbert said: "Master he be set on horses and so be I." So it was the dogcart that drew up at the front door.

Grandfather looked at the four children.

"How about a drive to Salisbury?" His eyes twinkled when he asked this because he knew they would say no. Driving in the dogcart meant going with their backs to the horses, and they were all sick that way around.

Instead of going they helped to tuck him in under his plaid rug beside Hibbert and they watched James get up on the backseat, and then they stood on the steps and waved good-bye.

At half-past twelve Grandfather came driving back. He climbed out of his seat carefully, then he turned to James.

"Give me that parcel." He nodded to the children and took a square brown parcel from James. "You come with me." His look included Dr. and Mrs. Heath and Pinny. He marched into the dining room with them all trailing behind. In the dining room the table was being set for lunch. Grandfather never cared about things like tables being set, and he swept back the cloth. The cloth upset the salt-cellar. Susan was shocked to see that Grandfather never botherered to throw salt over his left shoulder, so she did a little salt-throwing herself to keep bad luck from him. Of course she did not believe that salt really brought bad luck, but all the same it made her feel worried inside to see it upset and no precautions taken.

Grandfather, having made a space for himself on the table, sat down in his own chair, which was a Hepplewhite and beautiful to look at. He took the carving knife and cut the string of the parcel. First there was a layer of brown paper, then there was a cardboard box, and then tissue paper. Grandfather's fingers were a little stiff with rheumatism. He took a tremendous time undoing the tissue paper, but because of the stiffness and the rheumatism none of the children liked to say "Oh, do hurry up!" When the tissue paper was undone, that was not the end, for the thing itself was wrapped in a piece of cotton wool. Even Grandfather's slow fingers could not fumble much over cotton wool. He pulled off the last piece and took out what he had bought. It was a little silver house.

They all took in their breath rather loudly. The little house was mostly beautifully made. It looked a cross between the wolf-proof house the sensible pig built in Walt Disney's cartoon and something magic, rather like the witch's house in *Hansel and Gretel*. The downstairs rooms had bow windows. There were eaves in the roof.

The chimneys had a twisted look, as if they had been up a long time and had got rather blown about.

Grandfather looked at them all.

"Know what this is?"

The children examined the house more closely. They were not quite sure what Grandfather meant. It was obviously a toy house made of silver. If he meant "what was it for," that was different. Susan thought it might be meant for a very tiny doll to live in. Jim hoped that perhaps it had works inside and would be a clock or perhaps that kind of music box that has a prickly thing that turns round and makes notes. Nicky suggested that perhaps the roof came off and it was full of chocolates. David said:

"Per'venture it's for my farm."

Grandfather laughed so much at David's trying to use so long a word (for people at that date had not begun to get used to him being fond of long words) that he almost forgot the house. Then he remembered and showed them. He took hold of one of the chimneys and pulled it down. The children leaned over his arm to see what it was. The chimney was on a hinge, and when it was pulled back there was a slot underneath. The house was a money box. The front door had a real lock and Grandfather had a tiny key which fitted it. When the front door was open it showed that inside the house was hollow. When you put money in the slot under the chimney it fell straight through to where the hall ought to be. When you wanted to get the money out again you opened the front door and pulled it out onto the front steps, or drive, or whatever you liked to think would be there. Grandfather let them see this happen. He opened his note case and took out four one-pound notes.

"Here is a pound each, me dears." He handed them

around, and pulled back the chimney. "Come on, twins, yours first."

It was fun to see the notes come tumbling through, because although, of course, one part of you knew that the whole house was hollow, and that naturally if you put something in at the top it would drop to the bottom, the other half could not help thinking of the pound note sliding down the bedroom chimney and walking in a very dignified way to the door and along the passage and then, step by step, down the stairs to the hall.

"What's the money for?" Jim asked.

Grandfather pulled David between his knees.

"I was just going to tell you that. Years ago, when I was no bigger than Jim, I was given my first tennis racket. It was a funny present, for where I lived there was no tennis court. We had a house in a big London square, and Londoners, especially children, had no tennis courts or clubs in those days. I used to look at that racket and wish I could play with it. Of course I took it across to the playground and we used it for rounders and tip-and-run, but I always thought those games rather a comedown for a lordly thing like a tennis racket."

"Daddy gave Jim and me our rackets for our last birthday," Susan put in.

"I know, my dear." Grandfather lifted his left eyebrow at her and the red hairs on it stood out more stiffly even than usual; it was a way they had when he was interested in what he was saying. "That's just the point. I have an idea that you might be some good at tennis. It's fun playing a game, however you play it; but to be first-class! That really is worthwhile. But games cost money, especially in London. That's why I bought you this money box. It's where the savings can go which will keep you in rackets and balls and pay your subscription to a club."

Jim looked at the front door.

"Will we always have to bring it down here when we want some money out of it?"

Grandfather held out the key to his son.

"No. I'm giving it to your father. Put it on your watch chain, Edward."

Nicky frowned at the house, with her head on one side.

"What I don't see," she said at last, "is, who except you is going to put the money in?"

Jim lifted the chimney and tried to look inside.

"We know there are four pounds in. That's an awful lot of money. It will probably last years and years."

Grandfather shook his head.

"Wish it would. Four pounds won't even cover the rackets and the balls. Then, later on, there'll be tournaments. If you're going to be any good at all, you must play in a tournament or two."

"Tournaments!" They all stared at him.

"I say, do you mean proper ones with people watching?" Jim asked.

"That's right." Grandfather nodded. "There're all sorts of expenses. Four pounds won't last long."

"It won't, indeed!" Mrs. Heath agreed.

"I suggest"—Grandfather fingered the box as though he were fond of it—"that everybody put something in when they can." He smiled down at David, who was fiddling in his pockets. "Even if it's only a farthing."

"That's right." Pinny felt the whole conversation was most admirable. "A penny saved today is a pound tomorrow."

"Not always," Jim objected. "I've had a penny since last Saturday. I saved it because it wasn't enough to buy anything I wanted, and it isn't a pound yet, it's still just a penny."

Pinny smiled.

"It's been turned over so often in your pocket, Jim, that I'm afraid it's the rolling stone gathering no moss."

"But rolling stones do," Jim argued. "I saw a stone once—"

"Never mind, son," Dr. Heath interrupted. "I think I heard the bell for your dinner."

They all turned to go, then Susan came back.

"Thank you for the house, Grandfather. What shall we call it?"

He looked at it thoughtfully.

"I don't know. What do you think?"

" 'Bella Vista' is sweetly pretty," Pinny suggested.

"It ought to have something to do with tennis or money," Jim pointed out, trying not to show how stupid he thought Pinny's idea was.

Susan clasped her hands at the back of her neck, which was a way she had when she got an idea.

"Let's call it 'The Tennis House.' "

The other three came back to the table. They turned the house around to make sure the name would suit it. They moved the chimney and shook it to see that the notes were still inside.

David finished examining it first.

"I think The Tennis House is an admirable name."

So The Tennis House the money box became.

2

The Practice Wall

You would have thought that with their having the silver house, something would have been done about learning tennis the moment the family got back to Tulse Hill. It was not.

On the journey back from Grandfather's, Dr. and Mrs. Heath traveled in one car and Pinny and the four children in another. This was because the train was crowded. In Dr. and Mrs. Heath's car there was a woman and five children, a clergyman, an old lady with an annoying cough and a canary, and a farmer. In Pinny and the children's car there was another family and their governess. They looked very dressed-up and affected sort of children, so, as the Heaths were in the car first and had got the windows, they turned their backs on them and played Who Can See the Most Cars? Susan and David against Jim and Nicky. They were so busy looking for automobiles that they never noticed the girl who sat next to Nicky. Ordinarily they would have noticed her as she had a dreadfully swollen face, and they would have wanted to know why. After they had been traveling about an hour, Dr. Heath came in to see how they were getting on. He saw the swollen face, and made a signal to them all to come out into the corridor. He told them he didn't like the look of that face at all and they were not to go back into the car. Of course, as they had not noticed the face, they had to look at it through the window, one by one so as not to be rude. The governess of the other children saw them looking and frowned, and made the child with the swollen face sit with her back to the corridor. They had all seen it by then, so it did not matter. Jim said he thought it was a bad tooth. Nicky thought a bee might have stung her. David said it was a " 'brasion." Susan told them they were all stupid; obviously it was something infectious or Daddy would not have fussed. They asked Pinny what made your face swell. Jim said he thought it was the Black Death, because he was doing that in history, but Pinny said "Mumps."

It must have been mumps because about two weeks later lumps came up under Nicky's ears. Although they hurt, she did not say anything about them at first, because it was the last day of Jim's vacation and they were driving out into the country for a picnic. She was very cross at the picnic and felt so awful all over that in the end she told Pinny about the lumps. Pinny told Dr. Heath, who felt them and said: "That little wretch in the train! Bang goes half a term's school fees."

In the end they all had it. Not together, which would have been bearable, but one by one. Nicky was getting up when David's neck first got stiff. Jim was feeling too miserable to speak when Nicky and David felt well enough to fight noisily. Susan could not swallow at the moment when a patient of their father's sent them peaches, so that the other three, who could eat perfectly, had hers as well as their own. All in all, an annoying illness calculated to make things like tennis houses go out of anyone's mind.

Nobody went back to school until the half-term. It rained a great deal and they got very cross. Then, just when they were at their angriest with everybody and each other, Dr.

Heath remembered the tennis house, and Annie took a share in making them well.

Of course it was not the weather to play tennis even if they had a court, and they could not join a club because Susan was still infectious. Then suddenly, one drizzly afternoon, Dr. Heath said:

"We'll get a table-tennis set. Very good for teaching you to keep your eye on the ball, and it will be something to do."

Opening the tennis house was quite a ceremony. The children half hoped some more money might have got in while they had been ill, but it had not. One by one they put their heads flat upon the table (except Susan, whose neck still would not bend properly) and saw the four pounds lying in the hall. Dr. Heath took one. They thought the three left looked like a lot of money.

Of course, as they were infectious, the children were not allowed to go into the shops, but their father left them outside while he went to the sports department. Jim wanted to bring a bell with them, and, while the car was standing still, ring it and say: "Unclean! Unclean!" like the lepers used to do, but he was not allowed to.

Dr. Heath bought a table-tennis set. They opened the parcel in the car and decided the money had been well spent. They drove home by way of Piccadilly Circus, which was out of their way but cheering after mumps. Altogether it was a very good morning.

They were not allowed to play much tennis at first because of aftereffects of mumps, but they played a bit and, though they were not much good, it made something to do. Because they were only allowed to play a little, they did not get tired of it as they had of rummy and things like that, so not being allowed to play much had its advantages.

25

Annie had been marvelous all the time they were ill. She had once had mumps and knew the not-swallowing stage, and she had been a great help at getting things down. Each day she had a different joke. The mere sound of her "Whoop, whoop, coming over" outside the door made life less depressing. The jokes were not terribly funny really, but when it is milky stuff in a cup which, apart from being nasty, hurts to swallow, anything which takes your mind off it seems grand. Sometimes she dressed up. Sometimes she danced while they drank. Sometimes she sang funny songs. On the days they were worst she did clown tricks. She came in very stuck out behind and then suddenly went flat. Another time she wore an old hat and a little stream of water came out of the top of it. They tried to make her tell how she worked the tricks, but she said:

"No. We've measles and chicken pox to have yet. We'll keep 'em for those."

One day, when it was too wet and cold to go out, when they had played all the table tennis they were allowed to, when every other game anybody suggested they knew they would hate, Annie put her head around the door.

"My! You look like freaks in a show. Get taken on anywhere as the longest faces in England. Why don't you play something?"

"We mayn't play any more table tennis," Susan explained, "because of our glands."

"Well, what about us making toffee?" Annie suggested.

There was a tremendous rush at this. Toffee-making is, of course, always a nice thing to do, but with Annie it was especially fun. She would pull out long strands of toffee before it had quite set and explain with it how trapeze acts were done. She had a sneaking hope that perhaps she might talk one of them into taking up circus work

26

as a career. Today, as they were feeling miserable, she was especially talkative.

"There's nothin' like the circus," she said, heaving a spoonful of toffee over. "You should see us in the early morning moving on. The smell of the breakfast cooking. The sounds of the men loading. The steam being got up on the old trailer."

"And I suppose a lot of animal noises?" Jim took a little bit of toffee off the spoon and licked his finger. "Growls from lions, and things like that?"

Annie stopped stirring and looked at him very scornfully.

"Lions! Your ignorance, Jim! There aren't no lions nor no tigers in a circus! 'Cats,' that's what we call 'em."

Susan pulled her arm.

"Did they have 'cats' down below while you were doing your act?"

Annie went back to her stirring.

"I never traveled with 'cats,' not more than once. The last turn, they are, on account of fixing the cage and that. Maybe I'd be doing me act when they were being set. What'd I care up in the air?"

David looked into the saucepan to see how the toffee was doing.

"By grabitation you might fall."

"Grab nothing," said Annie, who did not even know the word pronounced properly. "Fall, indeed! Why, I could hang upside down a week and never drop."

Nicky stood on one leg and hopped around the kitchen table on the other.

"But you couldn't now?"

"Bet I could. Not a week, because of me work. But upside down never did mean anything to me nor never will." She passed the spoon she was using to Susan. "You

27

keep that goin'. Now wait a minute while I find a bit of elastic."

Nicky stopped hopping.

"We've no elastic strong enough to hold you."

"Hold me!" Annie sniffed scornfully. "What's the matter with me feet holding me?" She found a length of elastic in a cup on the dresser. "Here we are."

Susan looked up from her stirring.

"If it's not to hold you up, what do you want elastic for?"

"Me skirts." Annie tied the elastic around the bottom of her skirts. "Used to do a double somersault in our act. Pink tarlatan and tights I wore. Used to keep an elastic around me waist and push it down. Looked better, Dad always said." She went over to the door, put a chair against it, stood on her hands, and hung on to the top of the door by her feet. "Take away the chair, Jim." She grinned at them. "This is where rightly there ought to be a roll on the drums."

Annie had to come down again because of the toffee, but they saw she had spoken the truth and really did not mind which way up she was.

David examined the door.

"It looks as though us could do that."

Annie laughed, and poured the toffee into a can.

"So you could, too, and a lot more besides."

Susan sat on the table.

"Could we? Would you teach us?"

"I would that. Bit of patter dancing, too, you might learn. Not to mention juggling with three balls. Maybe that's where we better start. The other two might be rough on your glands."

Juggling was where they started. They did not begin with three balls, of course, but with one. Annie said she had learned a lot of juggling from some cousins who were in the business. Her father had told Annie to learn all she could of it, as it was a fine training for the eye.

"And I should think it was." Annie caught the balls nimbly as she talked. "I'd go over to them for a bit of dinner on a Sunday, and sudden he'd say: 'Comin' over!' and before you knew where you was there'd be ten or twelve plates skimming at you."

"Didn't you ever break any?" asked Susan. She sighed enviously, thinking how much more amusing meals would be, eaten like that.

"No. They wouldn't break. Tin they was. Lost a front tooth, though, I did. Dad said he was glad of it. It would be a lesson to me not to take me eye off what I was doin'."

Annie's dad's views about the necessity of having your eye fixed on what you were doing were deeply embedded in Annie. The children found learning to juggle with a ball was fun, but sometimes it was more like lessons. Annie, bred to the circus, had spent her childhood at practice and yet more practice, and expected the children to do the same. She had them in a row in front of her in the afternoon and was very severe if they had not improved since the day before.

"Now, Jim, a couple of hours in the big top wouldn't hurt you in the morning. That's the sixth time you've dropped that ball.

"If you want to play marbles on the floor, David, no need to do it in my kitchen. This is jugglin' what's goin' on here.

"That's better, Susan. No need to frown at it like that, though. A smile won't hurt you.

"All right, Nicky, we all know you can do it. But I seen many a good artist crash because it seemed to come natural. Nothin' don't come natural. You may 'ave the gift, but there ain't nothin' but knowin' your job what stands behind you."

When their health got better she added to her lesson a few steps in patter dancing. All the children were clumsy at this, but they liked doing it. They had to be stopped from practicing when the patients were about, the tapping made such a noise.

The day before Jim went back to school Annie hung each of them upside down on the door. They came down very red in the face, not really having liked it much, but of course nobody said so.

What with table tennis, juggling, patter dancing, and hanging upside down, as well as all the usual Christmas things, including going to Olympia with Annie and meeting a clown whom she knew, nobody thought about the tennis house in the Christmas holidays.

It was Easter vacation when the twins had their letter from Grandfather:

My dear Twins,

Looking around the shops for something for your tenth birthdays, which, unless I am much mistaken, will soon be here, I remembered the tennis house. How is it doing? I hope you are all practicing hard and putting in plenty of pennies. I enclose a pound to help.

Your affectionate
Grandfather

P.S. Please tell David I am glad he liked the trucks for his train. Tell him now he is five I shall expect a letter written by himself. I am glad he had a nice birthday.

Jim and Susan opened this letter between them. When letters came addressed to them both they opened them fairly. Susan slit one side of the envelope flap and Jim the other. Susan took the letter out. Jim straightened it. Susan read the first line, Jim the second, and so on down to the end. They had read joint letters like that ever since they could read at all, so they did it now without thinking. They read the letter out loud and everybody looked ashamed except David, who was annoyed by the postscript.

"I can write," he said angrily. "But I s'pose a gennelman can keep a sectary for his corspondant."

Nobody paid any attention to him. They were all thinking how mean they had been about the house. Five pounds in all for it, and every penny provided by Grandfather. Nothing even done about learning tennis except practice at the table kind.

Susan looked worried.

"Poor Grandfather! What a shame! If Jim and I get birthday money, we'll put some in. Won't we, Jim?"

Jim nodded.

"Everything that's left over from my cricket pads."

Pinny looked up.

"I shall see what I can do."

"Oh, no, you mustn't, Pinny," Mrs. Heath objected. "Why on earth should you?"

"Ah, well." Pinny smiled at them all. "Many hands make light work, you know."

Dr. Heath got up.

"So they do, Pinny, bless you. But much more important than the money is the tennis practice. We've been slacking. I shall put that right today. Who'd like to come with me to Nobby's after lunch?" He knew the answer before he asked the question. All the children liked going to Nobby's.

31

Nobby Clark was a carpenter. Nobody called him Mr. Clark, or Mr. Charles Clark, which was his full name. Everybody just called him Nobby. Once, years before, Dr. Heath had pulled him through pneumonia. He was really very grateful for being kept alive when he might have been dead, but he had an odd way of showing it. He was a man who looked grateful very easily.

Nobby did his carpentering in a shed at the back of his house. He must have cleaned the shed sometimes or the shavings would have been up to the roof, but it never looked as though he did. There were the most useful things to be had on the floor for the picking up. Decent blocks of wood that Jim, who was clever with his penknife, could make into things. Shavings of all sorts that if taken home carefully and painted, made grand bracelets and and necklaces for savages on desert islands and ladies going to Court. Sometimes there were things that had been cut off furniture, which, although it was difficult to know just how they would be used, were worth taking home in any case. The foot of a chair with a castor on it; a bit of a door; odd pieces that had carving on them. All the time the children were in his shed Nobby kept up a continual grumble:

"Put that down. Let that be."

They paid no attention to him whatsoever because they knew he could not want the things they took or he would not let them take them out of the shed. Sometimes he did stop them. Jim once found a most beautiful round bit of wood, shaped like a dog. He had seen an interesting bit of carving someone had made out of a piece of root, using its natural bumps and bits to turn it into a frog and a sort of gnome. He had thought that he might do the same thing with this bit, as it had a bump on one side. Nobby, however, took it from him just as he was leaving.

"Give that here, Jim. That's a bit what's going to make a ball on Mrs. Higgins's gatepost. Since they come into some money they've changed their house from Number 27 to The Cedars, and they want balls on the gateposts. Lot of foolishness!" Nobby spat into a corner, which was a way he had when he felt contemptuous. The children knew, of course, it was rude of him to spit, but at the same time they thought it was a grand way of showing what you felt.

That morning Dr. Heath stopped the car outside Nobby's house and they all went down to his shed. Nobby was sawing a length off a plank. His back was to the door and he never looked around. Anybody who did not know him would have thought he was deaf and had not heard five people come in. That was just his way. He knew anybody who was likely to call by their footsteps. Still sawing, he said suddenly:

"My rheumatics is cruel. It's all from what was done to me with my pew-monia." He spat.

"Sorry to hear that, Nobby." The doctor sat down on a bench which was against the wall. "I did my my best, you know."

Nobby nodded gloomily.

"You may have." He went on sawing and apparently noticing nothing. Then he barked suddenly: "Put that down, Jim. Let those shavings be, Nicky, messing yourself up." Then he added: "Some of us can't seem to do right whatever we does." Dr. Heath, who was used to Nobby, knew that this last sentence was meant for him, and not for the children; but he only smiled.

"Look, Nobby, I want these kids of mine to get some tennis practice. I thought of fixing up a length of board down that wall where we tried to have a rockery."

Nobby laid down his saw. He went to a flap of wood which let down on hinges from the wall. He used it as a sort of desk. He found an envelope and a scrubby end of pencil.

"What length of boarding did you reckon to have? Let that bit of wood be, Jim, that's the leg of Mrs. Foster's four-poster."

Dr. Heath took an envelope out of his pocket, on which he had calculations.

"Well, I don't want to cut back the currant bushes, which is one end, nor the lilac trees, which are the other. My wife is very fond of those. But I must have twenty-seven feet to start them off on the proper width. I walked it. I think I've got twenty-seven feet there."

Nobby gazed at the ceiling, looking rather like the frog footman in *Alice in Wonderland*. When he looked at a ceiling he seemed to be able to see other people's houses and yards.

"Thirty feet, easy." He spoke as if he had just measured it. "How high was it you was wantin' it?"

The doctor filled his pipe.

"Not less than twelve feet. Don't want to spend all our days going round to the next house to collect the balls. Even at that height we're bound to make a bit of a nuisance of ourselves. That's a lot of wood, I'm afraid."

The children gathered around to listen, except David, who was digging through the shavings in the corner of the room. His digging was rather doglike. He used both hands scooping the shavings out, so that they fell in a shower behind him. The others were suddenly anxious about the practice boards. From their father's tone it sounded as if they might be too expensive to have.

Nobby kept licking the end of his pencil and making tremendous calculations. At last he looked up.

"Those planks what I had over from Mr. Miles's garage would about do us, I reckon." He looked over at David.

"Steady, there, steady, no need to muck the whole place up." He returned to his envelope. "The wood. My time. Fixing 'em. Say twenty-five shillings."

"That's ridiculously cheap," said the doctor. The children sighed with relief and went back to nosing among the shavings. "There's no need to cheat yourself."

"Who said anything about cheating themselves?" Nobby grumbled. He put the bit of paper away in his pocket and the pencil behind his ear and took up his saw again. "Put that down, Susan. That's the side for one of her ladyship's new kennels. If you don't like the price, Doctor, you can leave it." He began to saw his plank in an angry way. "I'll be along Saturday," he added.

Nobby came on Saturday and built a practice wall. Of all the things he ever built he grew to be fondest and proudest of that wall. Years later, whenever he was passing, he would walk into the yard. Disregarding all such things as herbaceous borders, rhododendrons in full flower, the holly at Christmas scarlet with berries, he would make straight for the practice board. He would stand in front of it gazing at it in silence for a moment or two. Then an odd sound, which was like a groan but was really admiration, would burst from him:

"Lovely bit of work!" Then he would turn and walk straight out of the yard again.

As soon as the wall was finished Dr. Heath got some white paint and made it ready to practice on. The children stood around and wished they might do the painting.

"You can't," their father explained. "You see, I am going to paint a white line right across, just the height and just the width of a singles tennis court."

"If you drew it in pencil," Jim suggested, "I could put on the paint."

Dr. Heath shook his head.

35

"Not this time, old man. You shall next time. The paint's bound to wear off. Want to get it accurate to start with, so it'll do us for always." He measured carefully, and then painted a line right across the middle. "This is the net," he explained. "We've a singles court here. Twenty-seven feet wide that has to be. Posts ought to be three feet outside the net. We can't do that. Only got thirty feet."

"One and a half feet each side, then," said Susan.

Jim dug his elbow into her.

"Don't show off."

She dug her elbow into him.

"All right. Remember that next time you bring home a cup for swimming."

Dr. Heath was awfully happy. He loved messing about with paints and brushes when he had a chance. He made his net the correct three feet high in the middle and he painted two posts the proper three feet six inches. Right down the center he put in the line to divide the service courts. Of course, none of this was necessary: all that was needed was a white line straight across for a net, but he enjoyed fussing and measuring. It was the same fun to him that jigsaw puzzles are to other people.

When he had finished painting the wall, he painted a base line. It was not really much good painting it, as by the time the practice wall was up there were only forty feet of yard left. Of course, Dr. Heath painted the line its proper thirty-nine feet from the net, but obviously no-body could really serve from outside it as their racket would hit the wall behind them. All the same it looked very smart and professional when it was done.

It was getting quite late when the last line was finished. Pinny had come out some time before and fetched David to bed. They all felt, however, that their wall must be admired. Susan collected Mrs. Heath. Jim went for Annie.

Nicky galloped upstairs and told Pinny to look out of the window. All the audience behaved splendidly.

"You never did that yourself, did you, darling?" Mrs. Heath said admiringly to her husband. "It looks like the work of a professional."

"Never keep a dog if you can bark yourself," Pinny called from the window. "It's beautiful work, Doctor."

Annie looked at it with her head on one side. Then she nodded:

"If doctoring fails, you could get a job as handyman about a circus."

They all went in after that. They felt nobody could say anything better.

3

The Committee

It was a gorgeously warm day. The children were sitting on the steps into the yard waiting for their father to give Jim a lesson. Susan sighed.

"It's queer, seeing how hard we've worked, how little we seem to know."

"I don't know." Nicky got up. She took the racket from Jim and swung her arm back and then brought it smoothly forward. She held it out.

"Look at that. I should have hit the ball right in the middle, wouldn't I? You can't say I haven't learned something."

Jim snatched his racket back.

"Shut up, you little show-off. Anybody can do that."

Nicky sat down.

"All right, do it yourself. You couldn't yesterday."

Jim jumped up. He swung his racket all right and brought it forward just as Nicky had done. But somehow it was obviously not at an angle that would have hit any ball straight. Susan got up and inspected it.

"You'd have hit that one on the wood," she said regretfully, hating to side with Nicky against Jim. Nicky looked aggravated.

"Look at your shoulders, dear," she said pertly. "Both facing front."

Jim grunted and twisted his body so that his left shoulder turned toward an imaginary net.

"All right, you only know it like a parrot."

David looked up from the car he was playing with.

"Nicky has a nat'ral aptichude."

Nicky knelt down beside him and gave his car a little push.

"Have I? What is that?"

David took the car from her and put it back where it had been before.

"That car was doing seventy up the Great West Road. You mustn't move it."

Nicky turned to the twins.

"What's an 'aptichude'?"

Neither of them had the least idea.

"I should think it's another word for conceit," Jim suggested. "And about right too."

"It's a funny thing, you know"—Susan hugged her knees—"I never knew till the tennis wall went up that Daddy knew such a lot about games."

Jim picked up a handful of small stones. He tried to hit a daisy on the lawn.

"You knew he was good at tennis until his leg."

Nicky lay down flat on her back on the path. She turned her feet over on top of her head and held her ankles.

"I didn't know he knew much about all the other games."

Susan shook back her braids.

"I don't mean him exactly knowing things. I mean him wanting things. Of course, I knew he was Cambridge and liked them to win the boat race. But I didn't know he minded about England winning anything."

Jim had not managed to hit his daisy, so he picked up another handful of stones.

39

"I don't think he does really. I mean, not because it's England. I think it's because we used to win everything and now we can't."

Susan nodded.

"Daddy says English people used to win the tennis tournaments at Wimbledon."

Nicky rolled over on her face.

"I don't expect we ever did really. I think the Americans have always won."

"I get sort of nervous," Susan said anxiously, "that Daddy will get any ideas about us."

Jim hit his daisy and put down the rest of the stones and leaned against the step.

"So do I," he agreed gloomily. "I don't think anybody English has ever broken a world's swimming amateur record. I heard Daddy ask Pinny yesterday to clean my winning cups."

"Goodness!" said Susan. "You don't think he wants you to do it?"

Nicky giggled.

"He'll be very disappointed if he does."

David gave her a push with his foot.

"Will you get off the Great West Road! You've stopped my car."

Dr. Heath came out of the house. He looked at his watch.

"Sorry, Jim, old man, I did want to give you a decent lesson today, seeing it's so near the end of vacation, but the patients would talk." He went down to the practice board with Susan and Jim.

Nicky swiveled around on her behind so that she got off David's Great West Road. It was nice lying on the path, though the pebbles dug into her through her sweater, which was a bit uncomfortable, but not enough to matter. It was lovely to find a hot day. It had not been really hot since

40

last summer. She was glad that Jim was having the lesson. It was lucky that he had to have most of Daddy's time. It would be awful when the term began. She wished people were not so keen on stupid things. Why shouldn't you run with the ball at netball? It was much less trouble than tossing it up and down. As long as you got the ball back over the net at tennis why should anybody care how you held your racket? Even Annie was fussy, worrying about the way you stood to juggle. As if juggling could ever matter. Grown-up people were very silly. Always making rules that somebody had to learn. She heard Jim's lesson as though it were a radio playing in the next yard. Quite nice, but nothing to do with her.

"Do hold your racket tight, old man. It's swiveling at each stroke. Don't jab. Don't stand too close to the ball. That's it. Swing right back. That's better. You hit that one square. Don't forget your follow-through. Don't snatch at it. Stop a moment, old man. You must follow through."

"Why?" Jim's voice sounded angry. "When I hit it and it's gone, what does it matter what the racket is doing afterwards?"

Nicky heard her father laugh.

"It's just one of those rules. You'll have to take it for granted that I'm right at the moment. You can prove it for yourself on a court in the summer vacation."

"It seems very silly to me." Jim sounded crosser than ever.

"I expect it does, old man. Honestly, it's true, though. If you finish a stroke the moment you've hit, the ball loses pace, direction, and you've no control over it."

There was a sound of the tennis racket being banged on the grass. Nicky sat up hopefully, wondering if Jim was going to get into a proper temper. He looked as

41

though he might. His face was very red. He was beating quite a hole in the lawn with the edge of the racket.

"Well, I don't see. It's silly doing things you can't understand."

Nicky looked at her father to see if he was angry, too, but he had not seemed to notice that Jim was cross. He had taken his pipe out of his pocket and was filling it with tobacco.

"Come on, Jim. Let's have another try. Now a nice steady swing back. Mind your feet."

Jim stopped playing and looked at his feet.

"There's nothing wrong with them. And I don't see why it would matter if there were. You don't kick tennis balls."

Nicky wriggled a little nearer. She enjoyed other people's arguments.

"Well, have a look." Dr. Heath stood as Jim had been standing. "How can you hit the ball when you're facing it? You must get your left shoulder around. You can't do that with your feet the opposite way on. If you think all the time 'Are my feet right?' you needn't bother about the rest so much, because if your feet are right, your body will be."

"And if he holds his racket tight," Nicky prompted.

Jim glared. Her father turned to her.

"Jim is just as capable of remembering that as you are. If you want to watch the lesson you may, but don't interrupt."

After that Nicky tried to look intelligent. She did not succeed very well. It was not very interesting. Jim was only right all over about once in twenty strokes. Sometimes it was his feet. Sometimes his follow-through. Sometimes he snatched. To Nicky it was rather like hearing a person practicing chopsticks, playing it over and over again and always wrong. She was very good at chopsticks, both the treble and the bass. She always had a feeling when people played it wrong that she would like to knock them off the piano stool and do it instead. She longed to take the racket and say "Let me do it." Instead, she slipped off into the house while no one was looking. She went to the kitchen and had a long talk with Annie about seals.

The day before Jim went back to school the children had a committee meeting in the garden. They brought a table, four chairs, and pencils and paper for everyone. Susan knew this was right, because once when she had a cold she had been in the room while her mother held a committee of the Hospital Linen Guild. When everything was brought out she looked it over carefully to see all was in order.

"At meetings," she said rather grandly, "there has to be a chairman, a secretary, and a treasurer."

Jim sat down on the table.

"You aren't the only one who knows that. But do you know what they all do?"

Susan hesitated.

"Well, I was very little and I was reading *Peter Rabbit* all the time, but the chairman was the one that said what everyone was going to talk about. The secretary wrote down what everybody talked about. The treasurer looks after the money."

Jim nodded.

"That sounds right. Secretaries keep minutes."

Susan was puzzled.

"Minutes! Do you mean the secretary has to have a clock to see how long it is all taking?"

Jim was vague what minutes were. They came into talks they had once a week at school, called Current Affairs.

43

They were all about parliaments and things like that. All over the world secretaries seemed to take minutes.

"I don't know exactly. I think it's just what the secretary writes down is called."

"We shan't need to have a treasurer," Nicky pointed out. "The meeting is about the tennis house, and, as it has all the money inside it, I suppose the tennis house is the treasurer."

Susan retied the ribbon on the end of one of her braids.

"Well, we can't bring the tennis house to the committe—we wouldn't be allowed to—so we had better call somebody treasurer even if they don't do anything. I'm sure there has to be one, or it isn't a proper meeting."

Nicky hopped around the table.

"Well, I want to be the chairman."

Susan gave her a very odd look.

"Well, you won't be. The chairman has to be the oldest person, and that's either Jim or me; and Jim is by ten minutes, so it's him."

"Well, I won't be secretary." Nicky sat down at the table and drew on the committee writing paper a cat's-back view sitting on a brick wall with the sun setting behind it in between two mountains. "You all talk an awful lot and very fast. I couldn't write it down."

"I'll be secretary," Susan offered. "And if anyone talks too much, the chairman has to tap on the table for people to be quiet. You'll have to be treasurer, Nicky. And don't mess about on the committee writing paper."

Nicky drew three hairs on the cat's tail and laid down her pencil.

"Why can't David be?"

44

They all looked at David, who was kneeling on the grass mending a signal tower.

"David, come and sit down," Jim called. "You're part of the committee."

"Can I bring my signal?"

Jim looked as if he were going to say no, so Susan whispered hurriedly:

"He won't sit still if he doesn't."

"All right. Bring your signal." Jim sat down at the top of the table. Susan sat on his left. Nicky was at the bottom. David climbed onto the chair facing Susan.

"I suppose," Susan said, "I ought to write down bits about chairmen and things?" She began writing quickly. While she was doing it Nicky went on drawing. Jim got up and showed David what was the matter with his signal tower. When she had finished writing Susan cleared her throat. "I think this is all right. 'A meeting was held about getting more money for the tennis house. Jim was chairman. I am secretary. Nicky is treasurer.' "

"I can't see why David can't be treasurer," Nicky argued.

"I can't see why it matters who is," Jim pointed out. "You said yourself the tennis house is treasurer really. Now, for goodness' sake, do be quiet all of you. The thing is, how are we going to get some money to put into it?"

"Well, I thought"—Susan clasped her hands at the back of her neck—"there's our pocket money. Do you know how much we get? I worked it out last night. Jim and I have threepence a week. Which is a shilling a month. Which is twelve shillings a year. Nicky has two twopence a week. Which is eightpence a month. Which is eight shillings a year. David has a penny a week. Which is four shillings a year. Then there's Christmas money and birthdays and things like that. Shall we all vow we'll put half of everything in the tennis house?"

"Oh, I say!" Jim got rather red; he did not like to seem meaner than Susan, but he thought it was an awful idea. "Not half! My threepence doesn't do for all the things in any case. Couldn't we give the extras?"

Nicky drew a frieze of dancing rabbits. At least, that was what they were meant to be.

"I don't mind telling anybody who might be interested that Nicky Heath is keeping her pocket money for herself."

This from Nicky made Jim more amenable to Susan's idea. Nicky really was insufferable the way she would do what she liked and never cared what other people thought. He was just going to say something snubbing when David interrupted.

"I spend my penny on my farm at Woolworth's. I need a lot more animals." He felt this was all and more than he need contribute to the meeting. He slid off his chair and sat under the table. Obviously it was more comfortable down there.

Susan leaned over to Nicky.

"If you don't mean to put in money, what do you mean to do? Do you know Pinny is knitting sweaters for people? At least, she's going to when someone wants a sweater knitted, and she's putting all the money she makes in the house. And do you know, Daddy and Mummy are putting in all the bits they can save? The sort of money they used for going to the theater sometimes. You can't be so mean as to let everybody else save money to make you good at tennis and not ever give anything at all."

"I could." Nicky added another rabbit to her frieze. "Who ever said I wanted to be good at tennis, anyway?"

Jim and Susan looked at her in disgust.

46

"Well, suppose," Susan suggested, "we could think of a way of making money, would you help then?"

Nicky sat up straight in her chair.

"If you wouldn't all be so cross I would have told you something. I have thought of how to make money for the tennis house, and you ought to write it down in minutes."

Susan took up her pencil again.

"I might, but I'll hear it first. I'm not going to waste my minutes on stupid things."

Nicky leaned forward.

"You know that when they wanted money for the church last year Mummy had that bridge tournament in the living room? The one we helped put the ashtrays out for. Mummy made six pounds that afternoon. Why shouldn't we?"

Susan laid down her pencil in disgust.

"That's the stupidest idea I've ever heard. Which of us plays bridge?"

"I didn't think," Nicky went on quite unmoved, "we'd play bridge, stupid, but family games."

Jim tried to be fair. It was rather a good idea, but it was annoying that it was Nicky who had thought of it. It rather spoiled the meeting. The chairman ought to be the one to think of things like that. He looked at Susan. She was writing the idea down.

"What do you think, Sukey?"

Susan finished writing. She looked up.

"It's a good idea, but I see a snag. Ordinarily when people have bridge tournaments and things it's for a charity. Money for the tennis house is for us. I don't think we could ask people to come and play games for that."

Jim thought this over.

47

"Do you suppose that if you give people tea and prizes they mind where the money goes?"

Susan put her head on one side.

"I don't see how we could get any money if we give tea and prizes. You see, if we asked people to come and play games, it would be all the girls in my grade, all the ones in Nicky's, and any boys from your school that live in London, and just the children around here. None of those would pay more than threepence. If we had to buy tea out of it, and prizes, I don't see where the money for the tennis house is coming from."

Nicky went back to her drawing.

"I think Mummy would give us the tea and there'll be some things we don't want for prizes."

Jim looked at her witheringly.

"You can be a fool. If Mother has to buy the tea, she might just as well put the money straight into the tennis box."

"If we had the trouble of doing the party," Nicky explained, "anyway it would show we meant to put money in."

Susan scratched the whole of Nicky's suggestion out of the minute book, her pencil making as much scratching-out noise as possible.

"It was a rotten idea really," she said. "I wish I'd never written it down."

Jim rapped the table with his pencil.

"Well, come on. Any other ideas?"

Nicky looked very annoyed.

"The chairman is the one who says what everybody is going to talk about."

"All right." Jim pushed his hands into his pockets. "I will. If you'd agreed at the beginning to give some of your pocket money, we should have finished ages ago. I think the best plan is for each of us to agree to put in what equals half our pocket money for next term. Next term is thirteen weeks. Thirteen threepences is—" He paused.

"Three and threepence," Susan whispered.

"Three and threepence," Jim said loudly. "And half that is—" He looked anxiously at Susan.

"One and sevenpence halfpenny," she hissed.

"One and sevenpence halfpenny," he agreed, just as if he had thought it out for himself. "Then, Nicky, you have thirteen twopences, which is—" This time Susan wrote down "2s. 2d." very large on her minute paper. "Two and tuppence," Jim went on, "which means half is one shilling and a penny. David has only one shilling and a penny. Half that is sixpence halfpenny. David"—he looked under the table—"will you promise to put six pennies and one halfpenny in the tennis house before I come back from school next vacation? You get lots of extra pennies from people."

David sighed. Any extra pennies, even his pocket money, he had some difficulty in spending as it was. Pinny said: "Look after the pence and the pounds will look after themselves." All the same, he liked the tennis house and quite understood the idea that everybody was to help. He climbed out and stood beside Jim.

"All right. Six pennies and one halfpenny will be my oppert'ry."

"Offertory," Jim corrected. "And that's only in church. Will you give one shilling and one penny, Nicky?"

Nicky bit the end of her pencil and looked thoughtfully at the sky.

"I might."

"You must promise," Susan urged. "We're all going to. You know it needn't come out of your pocket money. You get extra money sometimes. We all do."

"I won't promise, because I mightn't be able to keep it. But I will try very hard."

Jim sat on one leg.

"I do think, Nicky, you grow nastier every day. We'll give one and sevenpence halfpenny each, of course, won't we, Susan? Would you put that all down in minutes and see how much it comes to?"

Susan wrote the sum down and added it. It came to four shillings and tenpence halfpenny.

"Four and tenpence halfpenny! As much as that!" Jim looked respectfully at her sum. Annie came out onto the steps.

"Whoop, whoop, coming over! Anybody care for a slice of chocolate cake? Your father says bits between meals are bad. But I say a little of what you fancy does you good, and seeing it's Jim's last day, why not?"

Jim got up quickly. He was tired of the meeting.

"Well, I think we had finished anyway, hadn't we?"

He only spoke to Susan. Nicky and David were already racing up the garden.

4

Eastbourne

Usually term time seems longer than vacation time. To Susan and Jim it felt longer than it does to most people. Some twins are quite unlike and do not care a bit how seldom they see each other. They were not like that. They never discussed it. They certainly could not have explained, but in a sort of way they only felt half themselves when they were separated.

It was easier really for Jim than for Susan. He had made a lot of friends at the school at Eastbourne. Susan had heaps of friends at St. Clair's, but school friends are never the same when you go by the day instead of being a boarder.

The worst of it for Susan was that she and Nicky did not get on. She really felt that Nicky ought to count as a little one and go about with David. Instead of that there they were, going to school together.

St. Clair's was thought a very good school. That is to say, it had masses of boards in the hall, with the names of all the people who had won scholarships and exhibitions written on them in gold. In the gymnasium there were even more boards, bearing the names of those who had distinguished themselves at games, written in scarlet.

Susan hated being conspicuous. She never went anywhere without trying to be as much like everybody else as

51

possible, at least on the outside. St. Clair's tried to make everybody alike inside as well as out. Susan knew outside she was managing very well, but she sometimes doubted if she was the real St. Clair's girl inside.

Stuck up in the hall over the platform from which the head mistress read prayers every morning was: "Who aimeth at the sky shoots higher much than he who means a tree." Naturally Susan knew what it meant, but she knew as well (without actually thinking it) just what sort of sky St. Clair's meant you to shoot at. Being good at work. Being good at games. Being a good influence in the school. Lots of other things which might have seemed part of the sky outside, certainly were not part of the one in. Music, for instance. Books or art in any form. Dancing was all right, but only as exercise. There was no harm in being able to sing or play an instrument, but being too fond of it was showing off. Reading books was all right, but you mustn't talk about what you'd been reading. That was putting on airs. If you painted or drew, you were expected to do it in the art class once a week and not mess about with it at other times. Caricatures, of course, were different. That wasn't drawing; that was being funny.

The school suited Susan. She liked being in uniform. Brown serge in winter. Brown checked cotton in summer. She was good at lessons and at games. In fact, she was almost exactly what St. Clair's wanted. It did seem hard on her, therefore, that before she had been at the school two years Nicky must arrive, undoing in a moment the good impression she had created.

Nicky did not really mean to be as irritating as St. Clair's found her. But she never remembered rules, and she never wanted to be like anybody else. Susan was terribly ashamed of her.

The school was divided into four houses. The marks of

everybody in each house, both for lessons and for games, were added together, and a cup was given to the top house every term. The result was that St. Clair's was full of girls struggling to get to the top of their class and to win their colors. In fact, almost all the school but Nicky. Susan did her best to make her try.

"But you must see how you are letting your house down by always being at the bottom of your grade."

Nicky would look exasperatingly vague.

"What house?"

"You know quite well it's St. Catherine's, Nicky. Your house captain, Alison Browne, is awfully nice. You're very lucky to be in her house. Such lots of people who were in it are on the boards."

"But I don't want to be on a board," Nicky explained.

Susan looked shocked.

"But think of all the girls reading your name in gold, while they are at prayers in the morning, for ever and ever."

"I don't see what good that would do me," Nicky argued.

As she had no effect on Nicky, Susan had to apologize for her when her house grumbled.

"She'll be all right presently. I know she's always getting into rows, but she doesn't seem to be able to understand about rules. She's awfully proud at being in St. Catherine's House really."

Susan wrote long letters to Jim telling him how awful it was about Nicky. But letters are unsatisfactory. Hers made her feel more than ever that she wanted him home.

It was about halfway through the term when the worrying thing happened. St. Clair's was not a tennis school. Lacrosse, hockey, and cricket were their games. Of course they played tennis and had tennis teams, but there were not enough courts to go around, and so it was never considered quite so important as other games.

Tennis in the lower school was only for the two top grades. Susan had moved into the lower of the two top grades that term. She found she did not care much for tennis now that she was allowed to play. Her father put her off, for one thing. He said he would much rather she did not touch her racket at school. That he was trying to get some style into her, and messing about with a lot of kids would not do her any good. Susan felt inside that quite honestly this was true. But of course she could not possibly refuse to play. After all, her only excuse was that her father thought the game at school was not good enough. She was ashamed at agreeing with him inside. It was in a way criticizing your school, which was not done at St. Clair's.

The tennis was rotten. There was no coaching in the lower school and they all slammed the ball about just as they liked. Susan tried to practice special strokes, especially her backhand, which her father said was very weak. She would keep up a running criticism of herself in her head.

"Look which way you are standing. Sideways. You can't take a backhand unless your right shoulder is toward the net. Don't spoon it up. Look at your feet, Susan. My good child, look at your left foot. Unless your left foot is behind for you to swing back on, how do you think you are going to take the ball? That was better. That was much better. Don't get too close to the ball. You took that one very nicely indeed." And all the time she whispered: "Follow through. Follow through. You idiot, you took your eye off the ball."

Of course it was splendid advice and was exactly what her father had told her. Actually very few of her strokes followed the advice she gave herself. She was not experienced enough to know the good ones from the bad, and they looked better than they were because the other girls could not return the ball. In fact, most of her practice came when taking a service.

At one of the lower-school tennis afternoons, the school tennis captain happened to be passing just as one of Susan's backhands came off. Susan did not see her standing there, or she would never have hit another ball. As it was, though of course she made plenty of mistakes, she was at least in the right position all the time. The next day she was sent for.

"Susan Heath, will you go to the senior prefects' room, at once?"

Susan got up, scarlet in the face. She knew she had done nothing. At once she suspected Nicky. What awful sin could she have committed that would take her, a junior, in front of the senior prefects?

"Who wants me?" she whispered.

"Ann Ford. Go on."

Susan, hurrying like a scared rabbit up the stairs, forgot that Ann Ford was the tennis captain and only remembered that she was a prefect. By the time she got to the top flight she had decided that Nicky, and probably she, too, as she was Nicky's sister, would be expelled. When she reached the prefects' room she was almost too scared to knock, but she made herself somehow. Ann Ford was sitting at her desk. She looked up as Susan came in.

"Hello! Are you Susan Heath?"

"Yes," Susan agreed apologetically, certain that the school would soon be ringing with the name.

"You've had some tennis coaching, haven't you?"

55

"Tennis?" Susan looked stupid, for it is very difficult to jump your mind from your sister being expelled to tennis.

"Well, haven't you?" Ann asked again.

"Yes, from Father," she agreed.

"I see. Well, I'm having you put on to special coaching. You'll get a chance to play every day. At the end of the term I'll come back and look at you to see how you are shaping. Might get you into a team next year."

Susan felt she ought to curtsy or something. This was, she knew, a most tremendous honor. But as she went down the passage back to her class she felt worried inside. Her father had said he did not want her to play at school. He would simply hate her playing every day and being coached by somebody whom perhaps he would not think very good. On the other hand, what would her house say if she missed the chance of being on a team, with all the marks that brought in? How dreadfully swanky they would think her if they heard that her reason for not playing was that she was being coached in case she might turn out what her father called 'first-class.' How awful to even suggest that any game at St. Clair's was not first-class. Of course, the tennis was not, and the tennis coaching was not, and everybody knew it, but it was not the sort of thing you could possibly say.

All the rest of the day she turned the problem over and over in her mind. Should she not tell her father and just be coached? She knew at once that was no good. Nicky would be sure to hear and tell him. She did hope her father would understand. He had been at school himself. He must know how the rest of your house thought about you if you let them down.

She had meant to tell him that evening after tea. She came in strung up to do it. But the moment she got into the house she was told something that put it right out of her head. Next Sunday her father was driving her down to see Jim.

In bed that night she remembered that she had forgotten about the coaching. But somehow, tennis and teams and things like that did not matter so much as they had. Nothing mattered really except that she would see Jim on Sunday. In any case they were driving down. If you are by yourself with somebody who is driving a car, it's the easiest time really to explain things.

The only thing wrong with Sunday was that they were to have lunch at the school. Susan had done it before and thought it terrifying. She supposed all the boys were not really staring at her, but she felt as though they were.

Sunday was a most lovely day. The hedges were full of honeysuckle and dog roses. The fields had so many buttercups in them that they looked as if they had turned yellow. It was so dry the cow parsley along the borders of the road had its leaves gray with dust. Ashdown Forest looked cool. Susan would have liked to get out and walk through the trees and among the gorse. There was so much to see after being at Tulse Hill that she left talking about the coaching until they were going home.

Jim was waiting in the school drive for them. He was most terribly glad to see them and would have liked to say so, but he never found it easy to say things to his family when they came to the school. School was school and family was family. You could not expect them to mix. So all he said was:

"Hello! You don't want to see the chapel again, do you? You saw it last time."

"No. I think we'd better go and pay our respects," Dr. Heath suggested.

Jim looked at his watch.

"Well, I don't know about that yet. Lunch is a quarter-past one. It's only a quarter to. What would we do for half an hour?"

But Dr. Heath said he thought they would not be too early, so they went in.

As a matter of fact it worked out rather well. The headmaster's wife, Mrs. Partridge, took Susan to wash and to do her hair, and when she came back she found both Mr. and Mrs. Partridge drinking sherry with her father, so she and Jim were able to get in a corner and talk.

"Dad gave me an awful shock," Jim told her. "In his letter he didn't exactly say who was coming. I thought he might be bringing Nicky too. It would have been simply awful if he had. She'd have been sure to say or do something frightful in front of everybody."

His talking of everybody reminded Susan of lunch.

"Am I sitting next to you?"

"Yes. I'm to move up to the end. On the other side of you is Mr. Partridge."

Jim did not really care for having his family to lunch. Susan was pretty and all that, and she looked all right in that green thing she was wearing. But somehow it made him shy, the other boys looking at his father and sister. Of course, it was not likely they would do anything wrong, but they might. Anyway, it was lucky they looked all right. He did not want to be like Lang last term. His mother coming down dreadful and fat and all painted up. She had left her lipstick on the napkin. Jim supposed that if a thing like that happened to him he would have got Dad to take him away. He was sure he could never have borne the shame.

Luckily, as Jim and Susan were shy, Mr. Partridge was

a very talkative person. He told them all through lunch about how he had been in Lapland. He was very interesting and the twins, in listening to him, almost forgot the rows of eyes down the table.

After lunch they went on the pier. Dr. Heath changed a shilling into pennies and gave them six each, and told them not to leave the pier, as he was going for a walk and would come back and fetch them. They had a lovely afternoon. The pennies lasted a long time in the game machines, as they used them for football matches and things like that where one always gets another turn. When they had used all the pennies up, except one or two with which they bought chocolate, they went and sat on a bench and watched a man fish. Susan told Jim all about the tennis coaching. At the end he said:

"I should think Dad's bound to see. He knows that if they want you to play in teams and things at school you have to."

Susan screwed up her face.

"I sometimes think he doesn't think it matters so much at girls' schools. I hope he'll understand, but I don't feel a bit sure."

Jim wriggled more comfortably onto the bench.

"Have you done anything about getting your money yet for the tennis house?"

She nodded.

"I've kept the half-crown I had on my birthday. Didn't you?"

Jim looked a bit ashamed.

"Well, I had meant to, and then Jones bought a catapult one Saturday. Not a bit like an ordinary catapult. You ought to see it. I bet if I had it here I could get that sea gull." He pointed to a bird that was so far away it was only a speck.

"So you spent the half-crown on it?"

"No. One and fourpence. Honestly, I think it was worth it. It's a handy thing to have about."

Susan counted on her fingers.

"So you've only one and twopence. You want another fivepence halfpenny. That will have to come out of your pocket money."

"I know. I'm saving a penny this week. School costs a lot of money."

"Well, where is your one and twopence?" said Susan. "Don't you think I'd better take it back to London and look after it? You might see another catapult or something. As a matter of fact, it doesn't matter about the rest of the money. I kept my whole half-crown because I thought we might need it. I'll put your fivepence halfpenny out of that."

Jim was just going to argue that it was not fair to her, but the man in front of them suddenly caught a fish. It was not a very big or important-looking fish, but of course they had to get up and watch and see if they could help. Lots of other people came to watch and help too. But Jim and Susan, as they were there first, did the real helping and the man noticed it. When the fish was safely on the pier he gave it to Susan.

They, and the fish, went back to the school for tea. They were not having it this time with the boys. Instead, there was tea in the parlor. A special table was set in the window for Susan and Jim. Mrs. Partridge only gave one look at the fish and then said:

"How about having that cooked for your tea?"

Altogether it was a perfectly lovely day. Susan hated to say good-bye to Jim, but she could not help thinking that it could not really be very miserable for him with people like Mr. and Mrs. Partridge. Extraordinary to have heads of the school like that. She could not imagine the head of St. Clair's having any fish you caught cooked for tea. If it came to that, she could not imagine having tea with her at all.

On the way home she told her father about the school tennis. Dr. Heath drove on while she was talking without seeming to listen; but she knew he really was, it was just his way. When she had finished he looked down at her and smiled.

"You and your St. Clair's. I shall have to take you away one day, Sukey. How being a proper St. Clair's girl does worry you!"

Susan grew red.

"Well, oughtn't it to? You do see I'd look simply awful not coaching for a tennis team, if I could coach for it. If I get into a team next year, it's a mark every week for my house and extra marks if I do well in the match. You couldn't expect a house not to want those."

"All right, my dear. Have your coaching. I quite see you will find life unendurable without it." He hesitated. "Though I don't know really whether it matters terribly what the house thinks."

"Oh, but it does, Daddy. You ought to have heard them when one of the girls wouldn't play in the hockey team because she wanted to ride." She frowned in a worried way. "You know, Daddy, it's awfully nice being taught to play properly, but it costs a lot, and I don't see why any of us should be any good."

He waited to answer while he passed two cars and got farther up in the line of London-bound traffic.

"I daresay none of you will. Your grandfather was good and, though I shouldn't say so, I looked like being first-class myself before my leg. It would be grand if one of you turned out an ace at something, and tennis

61

in our family is the likeliest shot. There was a time, you know, Susan, when English people were better at games than almost anybody in the world. I sometimes think that we are going backward. Don't think I mind just because of England—I don't. I'd like to see no countries at all but just one world with no frontiers. But there are countries, and I feel that the fact that England doesn't win now as we used to is a reflection on us doctors."

"You! Why? What can you do?"

Dr. Heath stared at the road ahead as if he could see a vision.

"We don't teach physical training nearly so much as we ought to. We are far too fond instead of medicines and cutting people up. I think every father and mother in the country ought to aim at making their children first-class in some line."

"But everybody can't play games, and, anyway, everybody couldn't win."

"Of course they couldn't, but they could try, and because they tried the whole standard would go up. Besides, games aren't the only thing. Ever hear of Amy Johnson, who flew alone to Australia in a second-hand airplane before flying was half as safe as it is now? When we read of people like her it does us good. We remember we had good people once, and will have them again."

"Of course I'd like to be really good, but I'm afraid I never will." Susan wriggled more comfortably into her seat. "You see, I don't like people watching me, and they would if I had to play at Wimbledon."

Dr. Heath laughed.

"They certainly would. Well, try and get into your St. Clair's team. Perhaps it will help your temperament, but remember, if I find you getting into bad habits I'll drag you out of it again by the scruff of your neck, whatever your house says."

Susan was only half listening. The sea air had made her sleepy. Presently her father said something about Ashdown Forest, but she must have been nearly asleep, for what she answered was:

"It was a lovely fish. We ate half each."

5

The Umbrella Man

Nicky had been having a lesson from her father on how
to serve. It had been an annoying lesson. For one thing it
was very hot. For another, she thought her father was
fussing as usual about things that did not matter. She had
done all the things she had been told. Thrown the ball
about five feet into the air, "smoothly" as her father
called it, and what in juggling Annie called "easing it
along," but it meant exactly the same thing. She had
stood properly, right around with her left shoulder facing the net. She had swung her racket properly. Each
time she had been told to stop and look where it was; it
was in a line with her left shoulder, which she knew was
right. She had hit the ball properly at least five times out
of ten. She had not even forgotten to fling out her left
arm to help her balance. Most important of all, not once
had she taken her eye off the ball except when the cat
from next door walked across the wall, and anybody
would have stopped to look at him. She had even remembered that awful follow-through. Instead of being pleased
and telling her how good she was, which Nicky considered was only fair, her father kept up a continual moan
of: "Your feet, Nicky. You're foot-faulting again."

Nicky argued that it was ridiculous. If she had to keep
on hitting balls hard she could not keep thinking about

her feet. She got very cross indeed. She had stood right to begin with—she was sure she had. Her left foot had started just behind the line and her right foot, of course, well behind that. She did not believe it was true that her right foot swung over the line before she had hit the ball and not after it. In fact, she knew quite well that it had not. What with the heat and one thing and another she would probably have gone on arguing for hours, only a patient called and wanted her father, and he had to go.

After he had gone she lay flat down on the grass without bothering to put on her sweater, which would certainly have gotten her into trouble if Pinny or her mother had seen her. She wished she had something to do. Something nice ought to happen every Saturday afternoon. It was mean Susan had gone out to lunch. She thought it was very unfair of Susan's friends to ask Susan out to lunch and not ask her. Even David would be better than nothing, but he was in the living room with Pinny, singing. She thought David's singing a disgusting noise. She thought it was very stupid of Pinny and her mother to encourage him. There he was going on and on:

> A pocket full of rye,
> Four-and-twenty blackbirds baked in a pie—

"What a stupid song!" Nicky growled. If you baked birds they couldn't sing.

> The king was in his counting-house,
> Counting out his money.

Nicky sat up. "Counting out his money." What an awful thing! Only two weeks to vacation and she had not got her one shilling and a penny for the tennis house. Of course she had not promised to get it, but she had meant to, really. One and a penny. Even if she kept today's money and next Saturday's and the Saturday after's, that would only be sixpence. Sixpence! Well, sixpence wouldn't be any good, so she might as well spend this week's twopence. She got up.

Just down the road from the Heath house there was a cake shop. It was not a very big cake shop, but they were allowed to go to it by themselves because it was on the same side of the road. It was kept by a Mrs. Pettigrew. The children always called her Mrs. Pettigrew when they spoke to her, but at home they called her Miss Tiggy Winkle.

Nicky went to Mrs. Pettigrew's and did as satisfactory a spending as was possible with twopence; just as she was going, Mrs. Pettigrew picked up a paper bag and put a macaroon in it.

"Something extra because it's a nice day."

Nicky walked back up the street eating the macaroon. Because of it she would have been perfectly happy if she had not been worrying about the one and a penny. Suddenly, around the corner came a man pushing a cart. At the end of the cart were balloons and those paper things that spin around: On the barrow were jam jars and at the far end some old clothes. Nicky went across to have a look.

"Why have you got those balloons?" she asked.

The man stopped his cart.

"Well, miss, I gives them in exchange like for the jam jars."

"Do you give them in exchange for the clothes too?"

"No, I buys them. Got a bit of a shop about a mile from here. I deals in old clothes."

66

"Do you mean you buy them?" said Nicky, surprised, for the clothes did not look worth buying.

"Yes. Now this pair of shoes"—he picked up a disgraceful old pair with holes in the soles—"I give twopence for 'em. When I have done with them they'll be worth eightpence anywhere."

"Will they!" Nicky looked at the shoes with more respect. After all, eightpence is eightpence. She broke off a piece of her macaroon. "Would you like a bit?"

The man shook his head. "Kind of you, miss, I'm sure. But I can't touch nothing sweet on account of a hole in me tooth."

"Why don't you have it filled?" Nicky asked, eating the piece of macaroon, feeling glad he had not wanted it.

"Filled!" The man sounded shocked. "Teeth will fall out when they're not wanted. I don't hold with all this messin' about." He was going to move on, and then he changed his mind. "I suppose, missy, your pa and ma wouldn't have anything put away they didn't want, what they'd like to sell?"

"What sort of things?"

"Well, mostly anything. Boots, shoes, gents' suits, a nice coat, raincoat, or an umbrella. Wonderful what I can do with an umbrella."

Nicky looked at the sky. It would not rain for ages. It was much too hot. Nobody would want an umbrella. Perhaps nobody ever would again. Umbrellas were never used much anyhow, because of the car. At that moment her splendid idea came. In the hall was a stand of umbrellas.

"How many umbrellas would you want for one and a penny?" she asked.

"One and a penny!" The man said it in the sad voice of

somebody who had never seen so much money. "Well, not less than four!"

"Four." Nicky thought of those in the hall. There was one of her father's, her mother's, and two frightful old ones that might have belonged to anybody. "You wait here," she said breathlessly.

It only took a few minutes to get back to the house. She opened the front door carefully. She seemed to have been gone ages, but David was still singing. She could hear him:

> So Binkie's the same as the First Friend was,
> And I am the Man in the Cave.

She picked up the four umbrellas and went back to the man.

The man took the four umbrellas and turned them over. His nose screwed up as though they smelled nasty. Then he nodded.

"Seein' it's you, one and a penny. Though, mind you, they aren't worth it."

Nicky thought he was the nicest man she had ever known.

"Thank you so much. It's very kind of you."

The four umbrellas were put among the old clothes. Then the man fumbled in his trouser pockets. Nicky was just beginning to be afraid he had not got one and a penny when he found it. Two sixpences and two half-pennies. He laid them on the palm of her hand. Then he untied a red balloon and gave it to her as well.

She was so pleased that she got quite pink. The man did not seem to want to be thanked. He picked up his cart and pushed it quickly up the street.

Nicky, knowing how easy it is to spend money when

you have it about, went at once to put it in the tennis house. She was just moving the chimney to push it in when she thought of something. The others were a very disbelieving sort. Would they believe her if she just said she had put it in? It was quite certain they would not. She must have a witness. She went to the kitchen.

Annie was making a cake. She nodded at Nicky.

"You know, I wouldn't wonder if something could be done with David. 'Little David, the Singin' Wonder,' or something like that."

"I think it's a horrible noise," Nicky objected. "Could you leave your cake a minute? I want you to see me put some money in the tennis house."

"For why?" said Annie, going on mixing.

"Well, you see, if I just said I'd put it in, the others mightn't believe me."

Annie wiped her hands on her apron.

"And no wonder. You're a proper twister. Come on, then, let's see you do it."

Annie could not deny that the two sixpences were real, for she bit them to see. The two halfpennies looked all right. When the money was safely in, Nicky gave Annie half a sheet of paper and a pencil.

Annie wrote:

I saw Nicky put 1s. 1d. in the tennis house.

Annie

It was still half an hour before tea, so Nicky tied the balloon onto the end of her bed and then went out into the garden again. She took *The Wind in the Willows* to read. She lay on her chest under the plane tree, and ate the cake she had bought with her twopence. It

69

was a cream cake, so *The Wind in the Willows* got very sticky.

Pinny, David, and Nicky had their tea in the garden. Nicky did not want much to eat because she was feeling very full. There was a chocolate cake, so Pinny was suspicious.

"Spending your pocket money on cakes, Nicky?"

Nicky nodded.

"Yes."

"Have you any left?" asked David.

"Of course not. Why don't you ever buy your own? You get a penny every week."

Pinny shook her head at her. "Now, don't tempt him, Nicky."

"Nicky wasn't temptin' me," David explained. "I'm buyin' a cow. I'm going in for milk on my farm."

Nicky thought proudly of her money safely in the tennis house.

"You shouldn't buy cows or anything else," she said severely, "until you've put your sixpence halfpenny in the tennis house."

David nodded.

"Six pennies and one halfpenny to be put in before Jim comes."

"Do you know when that is, dear?" Pinny asked.

David was only half listening.

"No."

"Two weeks and three days." Pinny smiled happily. She picked up the tray and carried it back into the house. It was nice to think of dear Jim home. She did hate any of the children being away.

"Two weeks and three days, and that, my good boy," said Nicky, "means you'll only get two more pennies before then."

70

"Will Jim be here after only two more Saturdays?"

Nicky wriggled happily. It was nice to see someone else bothered when she had just got out of her difficulties so well herself.

"Yes."

"Oh, my goo'ness!" David looked most upset. "I didn't never know it was now."

"Well, it is," Nicky gibed. "You'll look awful if you haven't got it, because you promised. Dreadful things happen to children who break promises."

David's eyes opened wide.

"What sort of drefful things?"

Nicky tried to think of something very frightening.

"Bears and wolves eat them. The bears eat them out of doors, and the wolves come pad-pad-padding up the stairs after they're in bed."

David looked at her doubtfully.

"You're teasin'," he said, but not with much conviction. "There aren't bears and wolves in England."

Nicky paused while she thought out an answer.

"Not always there aren't," she agreed at last. "They just come when children break promises."

At this moment Pinny came out to fetch the rest of the tea things. David turned to her.

"Are there bears and wolves ever in England, Pinny?"

Pinny looked at once at Nicky.

"Now, Nicky, what's this you've been saying? Of course not, David. Nicky's a naughty girl, making things up just to frighten you." She turned to Nicky. "Now you can help me to carry the things in. Evidently it's a case of 'Satan finding mischief for idle hands.' "

Nicky picked up a plate.

"It wasn't my hands—it was my tongue."

"Never mind which," said Pinny severely. "Pick up those

things and bring them to the pantry." She looked at the sky. "I think we're going to have a thunderstorm. I must be quick. If your father is not back soon with the car I shall fetch Susan with a raincoat and umbrella."

Umbrella! Nicky looked in horror at the sky. It was true it did look like rain. The sun that had seemed as if it would shine forever was gone. In its place were huge black clouds.

"Do you think it will?" she faltered.

"Yes, I do. Come on, let's get everything in. Come along, David. You had better play indoors."

In the house David sat on the living-room floor and arranged his farm. He sang all the time. Nicky pressed her nose against the window. It was certainly going to thunder, and that would mean rain. If only her father got back in time he would go in the car for Susan. Then nobody would think of those silly umbrellas. About half-past five the storm started. Crash, roar; crash, roar; and in between, sheets of rain. Nicky glared at the gate but there was no sign of the car. Presently the door opened and Pinny came in. She had on boots and a red raincoat. Over her arm she had Susan's raincoat.

"Now be good, dears," she said. "I shan't be long. I'm just slipping around for Susan with a brolly and her raincoat and boots."

Nicky flew up to her.

"Don't go. You might get hit with the thunder."

Pinny did up the belt for her raincoat.

"Don't be foolish, dear. The thunder has passed off. I had hoped your father would have been back to fetch her. But as he isn't I shall go. She's only got that little linen on. If they lend her things they probably won't cover her properly." Pinny went into the hall. Nicky

72

followed her. Since the awful moment had got to come she thought it would be better to get it over.

It came at once. Pinny went straight to the umbrella stand. Then she uttered a sort of cry.

"The umbrellas! They've been stolen! Annie!"

Annie dashed out of the kitchen.

"Well, what is it?"

Pinny, almost speechless, pointed at the umbrella stand.

"The umbrellas! Stolen!"

"Stolen?" Annie went and had a look. "Well, that's queer. They were here at the time the telephone rang for the doctor, 'cause I caught the handle of the big one on me apron and said 'Drat the thing!' "

Pinny ran about like a frightened hen.

"Who has come to the door since then?"

"No one hasn't been in nor out. The bell hasn't rung once."

"Oh, dear! Oh, dear!" Pinny sat down. "This is most unfortunate."

David came out of the living room, holding a sheep in one hand and a goat in the other.

"What's the matter?"

"You haven't touched the umbrellas, have you, David?" asked Annie.

"Umbrellas?" He shook his head.

"Nor you, Nicky?" Annie fixed a firm eye on her.

Before Nicky could think what to say, Dr. and Mrs. Heath came in with Susan.

"What a storm!" the doctor said. "We fetched Susan in case she drowned." He looked around. "Anything the matter?"

"Indeed, yes." Pinny held her head. "I was just slipping out to fetch Susan. I had her raincoat and her boots and I

73

went to find an umbrella and then—" She pointed dramatically at the empty stand.

"Stolen!" The doctor looked around. "Anyone been here, Annie?"

"No." Annie looked grimly at Nicky. "Before you send for the police, sir, I'd see if any of the family knows anything."

The word *police* was too much for Nicky. She dashed to her father and caught hold of his coat.

"Don't get the police. I took them. Only I didn't steal them. I sold them. You see—"

Nicky told the story of the afternoon. Everyone would have found it easier to forgive her if she had sounded sorrier. Instead, she kept saying:

"Well, who wanted the silly old umbrellas anyway?"

Dr. Heath hated punishments. He would not allow them unless they were a kind of canceling-out of what had been done. He said sadly:

"Nicky, you've got to be punished. On your next birthday and at Christmas, and the birthday after that, and the following Christmas, instead of a present, Mummy and I will put an umbrella in the stand here."

There was an awful pause. Nicky grew very red and swallowed hard.

Susan thought it was a terrible punishment. Mrs. Heath felt miserable. Pinny cried. Annie made sympathetic clicking noises with her tongue against her teeth. Nicky looked around. She hated people to be sorry for her.

"Thank you, Daddy," she said cheekily. "An umbrella is just what I was hoping I would get."

6

The Tennis Tournament

They were going to Grandfather's for the summer holidays. There had been some talk of the seaside. It was Grandfather's tennis court that settled the point.

Susan's game had improved tremendously. She had worked hard and had definite style. She had put all she had been taught at home into her games at school.

Jim had been playing cricket all the summer and had no tennis at all. He had done a certain amount of practice against a wall, and he had played a little squash, but of course his game was not up to Susan's. The summer term for him really meant swimming. What with that and practicing for the school sports, he had scarcely thought about his tennis. Dr. Heath hoped that by working hard with him every day he would get him up to a standard to play against Susan, which would be fun for them both as well as good practice.

There was another reason why Dr. Heath was anxious to get Jim into form. Grandfather had written to say that there was to be a junior tournament, in aid of a charity, at some houses a mile or two from where he lived. There were to be both singles and doubles. He thought Jim, Susan, and Nicky might be entered for the singles, and Jim and Susan could play in the doubles.

Dr. Heath was not sure about Nicky's being allowed to

play. She did not work nearly so hard as Susan and she had not Susan's powers of concentration. On the other hand, for somebody as small as she was, she showed flashes of remarkable brilliance. It was odd how often, without any apparent effort on her part, her strokes came off. He was convinced that only work, and work, and then more work could make you even passable at any games. Yet Nicky, who did not believe in working at all, could do so well. He thought it would be very bad for her if by luck and weak opponents she won a round or two in a tournament. It was the kind of thing that would make her lie back on her laurels for months.

Going to Grandfather's meant to Pinny a tremendous lot of preparation. Grandfather had old-fashioned servants. Pinny had an unshakable conviction that they were tremendously interested in the children's clothes. She pictured them peeping into drawers, taking dresses off coat hangers, looking at where hems had been let down, sniffing at signs of fade. The result was that any dress that was getting onto its last legs she dipped in dye, and refurbished with buttons. It was the same with the boys' shirts. If there was any sign of fraying, they had new collars and cuffs. The result was that for weeks, what with the sewing machine, the ironing board, and basins of soap and dyes, she hardly left the house.

"Oh, Pinny, dear," Mrs. Heath said, "you'll wear yourself out, and really it's not necessary."

Pinny, however, would not be put off.

"A stitch in time, you know," she observed, turning the sewing-machine wheel more furiously than ever.

As a kind of reward to Pinny for all the refurbishing she did she was usually allowed to buy something new all around. For the girls the material for a dress, and for the boys shorts or shirts. She always made a nightmare rush for herself of the last days because she refused to do the buying or making-up until the final moment.

"What's about will be worn," she always said.

This year she decided on a *Vogue* pattern of dresses for the girls. Two days before Jim came home, and only five days before they went to Grandfather's, she went shopping to buy the stuff. Mrs. Heath was busy at a committee. Annie was doing the house. So she took David with her, for there was nobody to look after him. They went by train to Victoria, and then by bus to Oxford Street. When they got to Oxford Street they got out and walked.

Shopping with Pinny was not very nice. She knew exactly what she wanted and she knew exactly which shop had what she wanted, but that did not mean she bought it straightaway. Instead, she went to at least four other shops to make sure they did not keep exactly the same things at three farthings less for each yard.

The day was hot and David's legs were short. Pinny held him tightly by the hand. They pushed their way through crowds in three different shops to the flowered linen department. This was a stuffy business and not very amusing for anybody. It was particularly depressing for somebody of David's size. Almost everything interesting to buy was above his line of vision. Not that it mattered really, for when he did see interesting things Pinny hurried him on.

At last, however, they came to the real shop which had the material Pinny wanted. She knew they had it because it was the shop that had sent her the pattern which was in her bag. But even when they got to the flowered linen counter and had sat down, that was not the end. Pinny might have a pattern, and she might know exactly what she wanted, but all the same she liked the shopman to take down at least twenty bales of different stuff in case she could find something she liked better.

David was so bored that he could not stop yawning. He did not exactly mean to leave Pinny, but he was not interested in flowered linen. Besides, a little farther off were things that might be worth seeing. None of it was really the sort of buying that he cared to do. But he saw things he would not have minded having. Things that would have come in useful for his farm or something.

In looking around, he suddenly found he had walked much farther than he thought. He had, in fact, got to the door of the shop. Outside there was a loud noise going on. He went to the entrance to see what it was. There were six men walking slowly up the street. Their heads were close together. They were all singing at once. They did not make at all a nice noise. One man, who did not sing, had a box, and into this a few people put money.

David had never happened to hear people singing for money before. There was a small barrel-organ with a monkey on it that he had given pennies to himself in his time, but that was different. The barrel-organ made a nice noise, and there was, of course, the monkey. These men made a horrible noise, and yet they got money. He was most impressed and amazed.

It must have been seeing those men and their money box that made him think of the tennis house and his sixpence halfpenny. He did not believe that bears and wolves ate children who broke promises. All the same, since Nicky had told him about bears eating you in the daytime and wolves at night, he had wished he had paid his sixpence halfpenny. Now he saw the perfect chance to do it. He sang far better than those men. Why should he not walk up the road and earn sixpence halfpenny? He no sooner thought of it than he started.

David was wearing gray flannel shorts, a green shirt and tie, and a gray felt hat. He took off the hat and held it out for the money. He started walking slowly up the curb, just as the men had done. He sang, *Matthew, Mark, Luke, and John.* He found it rather difficult to sing loud enough to be heard against so many buses and cars. Luckily he had rather a high voice and the top notes seemed to come out above everything. It was surprising how quickly people seemed interested. But they did not let him go on walking like the six men had done. Instead, they all stood around him. Of course, as they stood around him, David had to stand still.

When he reached the end of the song he held out his hat. But people did not seem to understand. Instead of putting pennies in it, as they had in the box, they clapped. David looked at them in shocked surprise.

"Men," he said with dignity, "what sings in the street gets money."

A lady standing near him laughed. She leaned down to him.

"Where do you come from, darling? Haven't you got a nurse or anything?"

David was puzzled. Nobody had asked the six men where they came from. They just gave them money. He looked around.

"Would you all put pennies in my hat if I sang again?"

They did not wait for him to sing. A lady in a purple hat with a feather opened her purse. She gave him a shilling. A man offered sixpence. Somebody else put in a handful of coppers. David was clever at money. He understood it perfectly. He looked in his hat.

"I don't want all this. I wanted six pennies and one halfpenny." He took out the sixpence and a halfpenny and held out his hat. "None of this isn't for me."

79

"Oh, but it is, dear," said the purple hat. "You sing so nicely. You can buy yourself a pretty toy."

David did not like her tone. She spoke to him as if he were a baby.

"I have toys, thank you. My farm I am making over to milk. It's doing very well."

The first lady, who had asked him if he had a nurse, took his hat from him. She looked around.

"I think you'd better take this back. I'll take charge of the gentleman and see where he belongs."

The purple hat and the man who gave the pennies took their money back. The lady gave David his hat. She took his hand.

"Let's go and have some milk and some cakes, or perhaps ice cream. It's such a hot day, isn't it?"

It was only now that David noticed a very nice thing about this lady. The other hand that was not holding his had a green lead in it, and on the end of the lead was a brown dog. He was a very little dog and very long. David pulled his hand free and squatted down.

"This is a very nice dog," he said. "Is it yours?"

The lady nodded.

"It's a dachshund."

"Oh," David said politely, not understanding what she meant. "What's his name?"

"Agag. I don't suppose you would know why, but in the Bible there was an Agag that walked delicately."

"What's walking delicat'ly?"

The lady held out her hand again and took his.

"If we walk up the street you'll see. You watch his front paws."

They set off up Oxford Street. The paws were certainly picked up very carefully each step.

80

"I suppose I couldn't hold his lead, could I?" David asked.

She was a very nice lady. She never said no if she could help it. She just passed over the lead without saying a word. David thought it was a lovely walk. He hoped people thought the dog was his. Presently they came to the first shop that he had been in with Pinny. He remembered it because there was a lady in a bathing suit in the window. She was doing a dive off a cliff. They stopped outside the shop. The lady looked at Agag.

"I'm afraid we shall have to carry him."

David stooped down and picked the dog up. Although he was only a little dog he could not hold him very well. It was because he was so long. First his front part and then his hind part kept slipping.

"Perhaps I'd better carry him," said the lady. David gave Agag up regretfully.

"It's not that he's heavy," he explained; "but he slips."

They went through the shop and came to a cool part at the other end. They sat down at a marble-topped table.

"I think strawberry ice cream, as it's hot, don't you?" said the lady. David supposed he was buying his own.

"I've only got six pennies and one halfpenny what I got for singing *Matthew, Mark, Luke, and John,* and that's to go in the tennis house."

The lady said that she meant to pay. She said she had not put any money in his hat, and the ice cream was instead. While they were waiting for the ice cream to come they talked. She asked him all about himself, about the family, the tennis house, and where exactly he lived. She seemed very interested in everything.

When the ice cream came it was so good that no more talking was done until it was eaten. It was not a bit like the ice cream inside a wafer which David had bought

81

from Mrs. Pettigrew's. It had real cream on top and a cherry, and pink bits inside which looked like pieces of strawberry. When he had finished eating David felt very full. He leaned back and sighed. He felt a lick on his leg. He looked down, and there were two very reproachful eyes looking up at him.

"Oh, my goo'ness!" he said. "His eyes is different. One's blue and one is brown."

The lady said she knew. It was all right. They were meant to be like that. He was what was called harlequin.

David thought Agag looked reproachful.

"It was mean. I've eaten all my ice cream and never given him none."

"I don't think he would care for ice cream." The lady looked sad. "Anyway, poor little fellow, he's going back to the kennels where he came from tomorrow. I'm going away to India. I couldn't find the right home for him."

David looked pityingly at Agag.

"Do you mean he hasn't got no home?"

"Yes." The lady stopped suddenly and looked at him. "I wonder if all of you—the twins and Nicky and your father and mother—would like to have him?"

David looked down at Agag.

"I'd rather have him all for my own self."

She shook her head.

"Dogs should belong to a family. You'll go away to school one day. It's nicer for him if he's everybody's. Come along. I'm going to telephone your father and then drive you home. We'll take Agag and see what they say. You sound to me just the home he'd choose."

They went out into the street to get a taxi. The lady said it would be less trouble to telephone from the hotel. It was just as they stepped out into the street that they saw Pinny. She looked the most sad sight. Her hat was on

82

one side. Her hair seemed to have come down. She was running very fast. Tears poured down her cheeks. As she ran she kept calling out, as though to a dog: "David! David! David!"

David ran forward and caught her around the knees. He meant to tell her all about the ice cream and Agag coming to live with them, and how he had sung *Matthew, Mark, Luke, and John;* but just when he was going to begin Pinny looked down at him, turned bright green, made a funny moaning noise, and lay down in the road.

The lady took them all home in a car. Pinny sat beside the window to get the air, as she said she felt "all coming and going." David, Agag, and the lady sat inside.

When they got home Mrs. Heath was in, and she made the lady stay to lunch. Pinny did not have any lunch, but lay on her bed, still "coming and going." David and Agag had theirs in the kitchen with Annie. Afterward the lady drove away in her car. David was sorry to see her go. But it did not matter much really because he had had his ice cream, he had got his sixpence halfpenny, and, best of all, there was Agag. Whichever way you looked at it, a most satisfactory morning.

Having Agag made the summer vacation nicer for all of them. It's odd how much most people resent going for a walk when it is just a walk and nothing else, and how nobody minds at all when it is taking out a dog. Owing to the amount of time that was spent on the tennis court, David and Pinny did most of the walking out with Agag. He was a dog who did much more walking on a walk than the people who took him out. He would run for miles, giving little short, sharp, excited barks. The barking was because he smelled rabbits. David always wondered if one day he would catch one and bring it home. One morning he found that catching a rabbit did not seem to be Agag's idea in barking. They met a rabbit quite unexpectedly sitting in the middle of a path. Both Pinny and David stopped and said: "Oh!" expecting to see the rabbit torn limb from limb. Agag seemed very surprised to meet face-to-face one of the things he had been chasing for so long. He paused. He looked at it. Then he stepped to one side and walked on with an apologetic air as if to say: "Sorry to have troubled you, madam."

The others teased David about Agag. They said he was nicer to him than to anybody else.

"I like him better," he explained. "He barks and I sings. And we're comp'ny."

Grandfather, who heard this, nodded approval, the red hairs in his left eyebrow standing out very stiffly.

"Quite right, too. Most dogs are more worth knowin' than most men."

Apart from Agag, the tennis tournament was the most exciting thing in the vacation. In the end it had been decided that Nicky should be allowed to play. The tournament was being held on the courts of four houses, the players being taken to and fro in cars. Everybody had to be under fourteen. Nicky was, of course, very much under fourteen, and Jim and Susan had some way to go.

In order to prepare them a bit for their first tournament their grandfather took a hand in their coaching. He could not play at all now, but he gave them a lot of advice. Concentration was what he talked about most. Keeping your eye on the ball. And, as well, tactics. He said it was stupid, however small you were, merely to return the ball and be quite pleased because you had got it over the net. They all knew enough about the game from what they had been told, and from watching each other, to be able to look for the weak spots in their opponents. It might be that they would come across somebody who was weak at returning a deep drive from the base line. They were bound to come across people who were weak in their backhand. They must try and return balls at lengths and to places where they were not expected and least wanted.

Dr. Heath was very proud of Susan. She was an ideal person to coach. She was so keen, she never minded how long she went on trying at the same stroke. She would go down to the court and get her father to send her ball after ball, which she would return, whenever possible, backhanded. She would spend any amount of time by herself working at her service. She would put down a piece of notepaper on the court and try and hit it when she served. She found the wall of the stable made a place to practice on. It was not so good as the wall at home because it had no line painted across it, but it worked all right.

Jim had a great deal to work at to be anywhere near Susan's style. He had, after all, only had that bit of coaching last Easter vacation. He had, of course, played about one time or another on his grandfather's court, but he had not known how to make strokes then, so he had not really gained much from it. Now that his father was coaching him and he got time to play hard singles with Susan, he suddenly became really keen on the game. He had the sort of brain that does like to know why. He still wasted an awful lot of his time in arguing. But little by little he began to understand. Quite often he knew for himself why he had gone wrong before anyone said a word.

Nicky was a little bored by the tennis that summer. It would be fun to play in a tournament, of course, but she felt rather out of things otherwise. She had her daily coachings with her father. She had a certain amount of games with Jim or Susan. They also played doubles, she and her father against the twins. This last was fun, although it meant a lot of running about for her, as of course her father could not get about the court quickly. At other times she felt a bit in the way. She knew Jim and Susan would much rather play with each other; that they thought it a nuisance having her there.

Nicky was annoyed by this. She was, after all, nearly as good as Susan and much better than Jim. It was ridiculous of them both to put on airs and suggest she should go out with David and Agag. She might not be eight yet, but she soon would be, and in any case she knew as much as Susan did, or nearly. She wished that you could be good at things without having to work so hard. In her heart she thought you could. She would be on the bank watching Susan, red in the face, slamming the balls all over the place. Sometimes while she lay watching she would make up a lovely fairy story about the tournament. It would be a day of tremendous triumph for her. She would win the first prize. Jim and Susan would come and talk to her the next morning and say:

"Please teach us to play as well as you do, Nicky dear." Nobody would ever dare say "work" to her again.

They all went through agonies of fear the day before the tournament. Suppose it rained! They need not have worried. It was a cloudy morning of the sort to make you nervous, but it cleared up before it was time to start, and by the time they arrived the sun had come out.

The tournament began at eleven o'clock. Singles were to be played before lunch to get them well going, and both the singles and the doubles in the afternoon, and the finals, if all worked out to time, were to be played after tea.

It was a very elaborate affair to understand at a first

tournament. The courts were at four different houses. The players had against their names the house at which they were to play. As none of the children had ever heard of the houses, they found it confusing. Susan, looking at the draw, saw she was playing somebody called Nancy Green at Fulford Manor. Jim had a bye, and then he was to play the winner of the bracket above him at Pinton. Nicky was to play Marion Hawthorne at Windlesham. The house they had arrived at, and where the draw was stuck up, was called The Grange. Very muddling, they all thought.

Nicky, who never minded where she went or who with, was quite happy to be taken with Marion Hawthorne and a whole lot of other children to Windlesham in a perfectly strange car. Jim would rather have stayed with Susan, but he did not really mind being packed into an old Ford with a whole lot of boys to Pinton. Susan, however, was quite sick with horror at finding herself collected, together with Nancy Green, and taken to Fulford Manor. On the drive she cheered up, for Nancy Green, who proved to be rather nice and exactly six months older than she was, said:

"I'm awfully glad we are going to Fulford to start with, aren't you?"

"Why?" Susan asked.

"Well," Nancy confessed, "my father and mother have brought me over. I'd much rather they didn't see me play. I hate people watching, don't you?"

This was what cheered Susan. She was delighted to discover such a kindred spirit. She agreed heartily that she, too, hated being looked at.

As a matter of fact they did have an audience, because there were only two courts at Fulford, and all the people who were waiting to play sat around and watched.

87

Susan won her match. She was a far more promising player than Nancy. But this would not have helped her, as she played badly from sheer nerves. Fortunately for her, Nancy played badly from nerves too. Nancy's badly was very bad indeed.

Jim was beaten. He was not a bit surprised. He had watched the match which brought the boy who played against him into the second round. He was older than Jim, about thirteen, and the best player there. He did, in fact, end by winning the tournament. Jim came on to the court feeling beaten, and therefore played atrociously. He felt very glad his father had not been there to see him.

Nicky, at Windlesham, enjoyed herself. The people who lived in the house sat around the courts in deck chairs watching the games. The girls who were not playing watched too. Nicky was by far the youngest player. Marion Hawthorne was the oldest. She would, in fact, be fourteen the next day.

When their match was called, Nicky jumped down onto the court. Marion. who was big and heavy for her age, lumbered after her. The grown-up people sitting around laughed, and called them "David and Goliath." The girls who were watching called out: "Don't kill her, Marion." They said to each other that they hoped the baby would be allowed to win a game.

Nicky had no idea until that moment how helpful she would find an audience. She knew all through her that everyone would be pleased at each point she made. She could feel them hoping that she would do well. It was Marion's service. She skipped to her place.

Marion served her first ball. Nicky's eye was glued to it. She returned it perfectly. She got well down to it, and put

88

it far out of Marion's reach just inside the baseline. There was a roar of applause and a great deal of whispering.

Nicky was beaten. She must have been. Marion was quite good and had played regularly for over four years. But Nicky, considering the short time she had been at it and her age, was a marvel. From that first crack of applause she was lit up. She remembered all she had been taught. She felt quick and light; not herself at all.

The players were asked to bring picnic lunches. Tea would be provided. Mrs. Heath had set out the family lunch under a tree. Dr. Heath helped by opening the ginger beer. The car from Pinton came back first. All the boys scattered to find their families. Jim looked a bit hangdog when he saw his father.

"I was beaten, Dad."

Dr. Heath went on pouring out drinks.

"Well, what could you expect in your first tournament? Have some ginger beer."

Jim took the ginger beer.

"I played rottenly. You see, he played just before. I knew he was much better than me."

"Ought to have given you a good game."

"Didn't." Jim took a gulp of his drink. "Just made me feel a fool."

"Have a sandwich," said Mrs. Heath. "You've got your doubles this afternoon. Perhaps you'll do better then."

Susan got out of the Fulford Manor car with shining eyes. She raced up to her father.

"Daddy, I've got through two rounds. The first one I played rottenly and I ought to have been beaten, only the girl I played against played rottenlier." She turned to Jim. "How did you do?"

Jim made a face.

"Beaten. Hope I don't let you down this afternoon."

89

"Doesn't matter." Susan sat beside him and took her ginger beer. "My goodness, I'm thirsty."

Nicky got out of the Windlesham car feeling very cocky indeed. After her match everybody had talked to her. All the grown-ups and all the other girls. She felt her family was very lucky to know her. She came over to them. They were talking and did not see her for a moment. She coughed.

"Have none of you noticed that Nicky Heath is here?"

Jim looked at Susan.

"I bet she's won."

"As a matter of fact"—Nicky sat down and took her glass of ginger beer—"if you want to know, I didn't. But everybody said I was most remarkable."

Jim looked sick.

"Everybody is very stupid to say things like that to you. And anyway I don't suppose you were."

"I was." Nicky almost sang. "I was, I felt it all over."

Her father looked at her.

"That's enough of you for a bit. Have a sandwich. Susan's won two rounds. Now, there is something to crow about."

Nicky felt as though a pin had been dug into her. It was her day. Nobody ought to take it from her.

"You haven't?"

Susan's mouth was full.

"Yes, I have."

"Oh!" Nicky said no more. She ate her lunch in silence. She was not exactly jealous of Susan. But somehow her having done so well took the excited feeling away.

Jim and Susan were knocked out in the first round of the doubles. They came up against a brother and sister who played a lot together. They did not disgrace themselves, though. They took the second set, and got three

90

games in the last. They played at The Grange. Their father, who watched them, was very pleased.

Susan went off in another car after that to Windlesham. She did not come back until nearly five. She was terribly excited. She had won her semifinals.

The finals were played at The Grange. All the other players and all the grown-ups gathered around to watch. Susan was tired, but buoyed up by the excitement of winning. She had played all day (except for the doubles match) away from The Grange. There had been a small audience all the time, but there were two courts for them to watch, and she had known no one, so she had not been shy. Even now she was not thinking much about the audience. Except for the family she knew no one, so they would not bother to look at her.

The other finalist was a girl of thirteen called Miriam. She was tall, dark, and looked confident. She knew everybody, and walked about, talking first to one group and then to another, before the match started.

Miriam and Susan walked on to the court together. Susan was new to almost everybody there. Besides only being a visitor to the neighborhood, she had, of course, played away most of the day. The result was that the moment she appeared everybody started to talk in a half whisper to their next-door neighbor. They asked who she was. They said how pretty she was. They said how well so small a girl must have played to have gotten into the finals. Those girls who had been beaten by her told their parents that this was the pretty girl they had told them about. In fact, there was a perfect buzz of conversation.

Nicky would have been enchanted. She would have felt that it was all friendly talk, that everybody was liking her and hoping she would win. Susan did not take the talk that way at all. She felt it was about her, but she took it

91

she was being laughed at. Something must be wrong. Perhaps the elastic in the leg of her pants had broken and one leg was hanging down. Had she torn her dress? What were they all looking at her for? She wished she could run away and hide.

Unable to forget her audience for a second, Susan played badly. She was so self-conscious that she grew stiff. She missed balls that any other time she would have taken easily. Miriam won the match with the loss of only two games.

Susan felt ashamed of herself. She came very apologetically to her father. He, however, laughed.

"You must get over minding a crowd, Sukey."

The man who owned the house came up to her.

"Well done, my dear. You must come and get your prize."

"My prize!" Susan looked amazed. She had forgotten there were prizes, and anyway would not have expected to get anything as she had not won.

She won a beautiful clock. Her name was called out and she went up to a table to fetch it. She felt shy and wished one of the others would have fetched it for her. But all the people were nice, and clapped so much that it made her feel much better about having played badly.

When they got home Susan and her clock had quite a reception.

Grandfather said he would take it into Salisbury in the morning and have her name and the date of the tournament engraved on it.

Pinny said she should make a point of always cleaning it herself. It was no good letting Annie handle a lovely clock like that.

Even Agag, on being shown it, gave it a respectful lick.

In fact, it was a very proud evening.

7

The Circus

It was a good thing the summer vacation was so nice, for the Christmas holidays were awful.

They looked as if they would be particularly good. There were quite a lot of invitations to parties. There were tickets for the pantomime, from Grandfather. There was an enormous pile of unopened parcels in the hall.

Jim had not taken a great deal of interest in the Christmas rush. He came home with a cold which made him feel simply rotten. He hoped it would get better, but it did not. On Christmas Eve his temperature went up. By that night he had measles.

Measles is always a hateful thing to have. Jim thought nobody could be more miserable than he was on Christmas Day. He was wrong. By the third of January Susan was so ill that she ceased to care what anybody did to her. They could wash her, make her swallow things, turn her over, and she just gave in, too wretched to resist. Two days after that Nicky started a most suspicious cold, which was clearly measles by the next afternoon. Even while they were deciding Nicky was certainly a case, Pinny heard David give a cough.

"I don't like the sound of that," she said.

She was right. It was measles. David had it worse than all the others because it went to his ears.

All of the holidays were spent being ill. Jim went back to school a week late, and Susan and Nicky eleven days. It was not much comfort missing school because they were in the cross convalescent stage. For Jim and Susan there was one bright spot. Partly because everybody was busy nursing David and they needed air, and partly because they were considered old enough, they were allowed to go about alone.

The London you see when you go where you are taken is quite a different place from the London you discover when you go about by yourself.

Jim and Susan were hampered by their lack of money for fares. In the ordinary way they could walk a lot, but now their legs had after-measles wobble. All the same, once they were allowed out alone they never spent a minute indoors except for meals. They had to be back for tea and were not supposed to go out again. But between breakfast and lunch, and lunch and tea, they traveled miles.

Twice they went up to the West End. They loitered about looking at the boats on the Thames. They fed the pigeons in Trafalgar Square with some corn a man gave them. They looked at Buckingham Palace and wondered what the sentries would do if they tried to walk through the gates. They stood and watched some acrobats entertain a matinée line. In fact, they just meandered round getting the feel and smell of the place.

"Next vacation, Sukey," Jim said, "we'll go to the other parts. I want to see the docks. And there are exhibitions and things which don't cost much. We can just go."

Susan sighed with satisfaction. She had always hated the idea of growing up. There was something frightening about it. Yet now there were advantages she had never imagined.

"It's odd. I never thought of us doing this. Of course, I knew we could go where we liked when we grew up, but not now, somehow."

Jim considered a moment.

"I suppose it's the measles, and David needing looking after. Anyway, it's luck."

Their luck did not hold every day. Sometimes they were told to take Nicky with them. Having Nicky meant just a walk. Walks were all right, and they took Agag, which cheered things up. But being three spoiled talking.

They tried not to let Nicky feel she was not wanted, but they did not succeed very well, and this made her deliberately annoying. The walks were usually one long argument.

"Don't walk in the road, Nicky."

"Thank you, Jim. It's kind of you to bother about me."

"It's not you I'm bothering about, it's Agag. If you walk in the road, he does too. He might get run over."

Susan, anxious to avoid a row, would break in. She and Jim would talk about something for a bit. Then suddenly Nicky would start to sing. Jim would glare at her.

"Do shut up! You can't make that noise in the road."

Nicky would stop singing for a moment.

"If nobody talks to me, I must do something." Then she would sing again.

Or, at other times, if the twins talked to each other, she would have a loud conversation with Agag.

"It's very nice for us, Agag, having each other, as nobody else speaks to us. You'd hardly think we were their sister and their dog, would you?"

They were all quite glad when they were clear of infection and allowed to go back to school. It had been a wretched Christmas and was best forgotten.

Easter vacation was a different matter.

The twins' birthday came at the beginning of the summer term. This year they had an early present. They had a letter from Grandfather on the first day of the holidays.

My dear Twins,

As you will, I think, be eleven quite shortly, it is time you joined a tennis club. I hear there are excellent covered courts in your neighborhood on which, for one guinea a year, you may play from Monday till Friday. I expect the tennis house is in a poor way, since I noticed three new rackets last summer, so I enclose a check for two guineas.

Your affectionate
Grandfather

Grandfather was quite right. The tennis house was in a poor way. As a matter of fact, it was in debt. There had been in it Grandfather's first four pounds; then his one pound that came at Easter. There was the four shillings and tenpence halfpenny from the children. They had meant to put more in at Christmas but, having measles, they felt they needed their money for other things. There were two guineas Dr. Heath got from a patient, which he looked on as a present as he had knocked it off as a bad debt. There were two ten-shilling notes Pinny had earned knitting jumpers for nurses at the hospital. There was one pound eighteen shillings and sixpence, put in by Dr. and Mrs. Heath out of what they called their odd money. All this, of course, came to ten pounds five shillings and fourpence halfpenny. But out of the front door had gone: the money for the table tennis set. One pound five shillings for Nobby's wall. They had used the twins' original rackets until they were not worth restringing. Before they had gone to Grandfather's, Dr. Heath (who knew someone from whom he could buy wholesale) bought three really good rackets. They had also bought a dozen used balls. As well, the house was in debt. When the three rackets were bought an IOU was put in for David. It was signed by Dr. Heath for the house. It said:

"IOU David. One tennis racket. When you require a racket it shall be purchased before satisfying any other tennis need in the family."

There would be some more money put in the house, but not nearly enough to join a club. Grandfather's present could not have come at a better moment. The twins were so glad he had not just sent the money for the house, but had said how it was to be spent. If it had gone into the house, it would have belonged to them all and could not very well have been used as club subscriptions for two.

The covered-courts club made them feel very grand. From the moment you passed the MEMBERS ONLY written on the gate you felt in a world of real tennis. There were three boards in the hall looking like the boards in the hall at St. Clair's. On one board were the names of the boys and girls who had won the club junior championships. There were some such distinguished names among them that Jim and Susan, reading them for the first time, could only nudge each other and stare. It seemed magnificent to belong to a club where people like that had once played.

There were three hard courts. Of course there were a lot of members to play on them. When you had finished a set you booked one of the others for later on. Waiting about did not matter, for there was a lovely big lounge, with lots of armchairs and newspapers. There was also table tennis. There was a place where you could get tea and things to eat. The twins were not there at teatime, but sometimes when funds allowed they had glasses of lemonade.

The whole of that holiday the twins went to their club every day, except Saturdays and Sundays, which were not included in their subscriptions. They had to come home to meals, and they had to be out of doors for two hours, unless it was raining. They never spent less than three hours a day in the club. Sometimes their father went down with them for half an hour. There was a gallery on one side of the courts. He would go up and sit and watch them and take notes. Driving home, he would tell them a few of the things they did wrong.

"No good having a smashing first service, Jim, if it never comes off. Just a lot of wasted energy. Besides, it means you play safe with your second ball and just tap it over. Better work at something less ferocious that comes off the first time.

"You could both do with a daily quarter of an hour's practice against the wall. All your strokes want working at. As for you, Jim, it wouldn't hurt you to give a week to it—you're still running all around the ball rather than taking it on your backhand.

"It is stupid to slash about on a court all day thinking of nothing but who's winning. Keep looking at yourself. Feel where you're going wrong. It's a pity to give up your wall practice. No need to go to the club every day just because you belong to it. Keep an eye on yourselves, or you'll turn your faults into habits."

Nicky was disgusted with the whole way life was going. She had always fought against being classed with David as "the little ones." Now it was David or nobody.

"I do think it's mean, Daddy," she grumbled, "not to join me to the tennis club too."

Dr. Heath laughed.

"Tennis clubs are not for babies."

Nicky was very cross.

"I shall be nine next October. That's not a baby. Even last summer, when I wasn't even eight, I was allowed to play in a tennis tournament. So I should think I'd be old enough for a club now."

"My dear Nicky, playing pat-ball at a local tournament with a lot of kids who don't know how to hold a racket, is a different thing from joining a club."

Nicky looked at him out of the corner of her eye.

"You didn't call it pat-ball when Susan won a clock."

He ruffled her hair.

"Maybe I didn't. But you are not joining the club, which I take it is what we are really discussing. For one thing, I can't afford it. The twins' joining was a present from Grandfather."

Nicky thought a moment.

"If you and Grandfather gave me next year's birthday presents now, I could join."

"You could not. Not if you had a hundred birthday presents. As a matter of fact, as far as my present is concerned, aren't there two more umbrellas owing?"

That was the end of the discussion. Nicky said no more. It did seem awful to think of two more umbrellas. She had not realized it would take so long. It was mean, when all she got for them had been one shilling and a penny. She tried her mother next.

She found her arranging flowers. Someone had sent her a box of daffodils.

"Mummy!" Nicky picked up one of the daffodils. "I was wondering if there was any way I could earn some money?"

"What for?" Mrs. Heath popped a daffodil into her vase and stood back to look at the effect.

"I want to join the tennis club."

Mrs. Heath took the daffodil from her.

"Don't kill the poor flower. The tennis club!" She smiled at Nicky. "You are much too small, darling. We hope perhaps to manage it in a year's time."

"A year!" Nicky looked shocked. "Why, I might be dead."

"I don't think so. You don't look a bit like dying. Talking of tennis, run up to Pinny and tell her I'm going out, and ask if she wants some buttons for Susan's tennis outfits."

Pinny was at the sewing machine. She said she had enough buttons. Nicky yelled this news over the stairs to her mother. She came back to Pinny.

"Have you saved much money, Pinny?"

"No, dear. Hardly any. I've a little put into a savings bank. It will pay me a lump sum when I'm sixty-five. Why?"

"I was just wondering." Nicky spun the cotton reel around on the top of the machine. "It's dull with the others out all day."

Pinny came to the end of the seam she was machining. She took up the dress and examined it.

"Well, dear, we reap as we sow, you know. I daresay, if the truth were to be told, you are not very good when you go out with them."

"All the same, it is dull." Nicky caught her finger in the cotton and unthreaded it. She laid the end beside the needle, hoping Pinny would not notice. "I wish I could join the tennis club."

Pinny saw her needle was unthreaded.

"Oh, dear! Look what you've done. And my eyes aren't what they were. Don't fidget with the machine. Join the tennis club, did you say? I'm sure your dear daddy and mummy would never hear of it. You are much too small to be wandering about alone. I personally never have a minute's peace while the twins are out. But you! Indeed no. Most unwise."

Nicky, growing more dispirited every minute, went into the kitchen. Annie was washing dishcloths. They smelled very nasty. She looked up.

"Hello! Look what the cat's brought in. You've a face as long as a wet week. What's the matter?"

She sounded friendly and nice. It was too much for Nicky. She burst into tears.

"It's the beastly tennis club. The others go all the time. There's no one for me but David, and he sings all day and plays farms and—"

"There." Annie came and knelt beside her. She put her arms around her. "It is dull for you, and that's a fact. Why don't you come in to me more? I might teach you a bit of cookin'."

"I don't want to cook," Nicky wailed. "I'd rather do more juggling and patter dancing."

"Come on, then, let's dance a breakdown. Nothing like it for raisin' the spirits."

Annie whistled. Then she began to dance. Presently Nicky joined in. They finished with a kind of cakewalk round the kitchen. When they were done they were both so out of breath, they fell exhausted into two chairs.

"You do that nice," Annie panted. "Funny kid, you are. You can do anything you put your mind to."

"I know that bit. Could you teach me some more, and some more juggling? Just me, while the others are at that club?"

Annie laughed. She got up and fetched bowls and things to make cakes.

"I've taught you most all of what I ever knew. 'Tisn't

101

like as if it was my own stuff. It's only what I picked up from the other acts when I was a kid."

Nicky eyed the bowl hopefully.

"Are you going to make cakes?"

Annie nodded.

"Just a dripping one for your tea."

Nicky helped herself to a little bit of dripping. She licked it off the end of her finger.

"I suppose you learned a lot of things from the other acts?"

Annie shook her head.

"No. Not learned. Just got a smattering. That's very different. Learning's what you're doing out there with the doctor on Nobby's wall. I like to hear your father. Keeps at it same as Dad done to me. When I hear him going on at you to do the same thing over and over, I say to meself: 'That's the stuff.'"

Nicky sat on the table where she could watch the mixing better.

"But you were learning to do it properly. That's different."

"And what are you learning for? Fun? The doctor thinks different. Do it well if you're goin' to do it, he says, and I reckon he's right."

Nicky sighed.

"It's all right for Susan. She liked practicing. Besides, Daddy says she might play well. He never says that to me. He doesn't even let me join a club."

Annie stopped working. She leaned on the table and put her face close to Nicky's.

"I tell you this, Nicky Heath. No matter what the doctor says, nor nobody else, you could do as well as Susan, and better, if you'd work. I seen it happen over and over again. All may start the same. All learn their stuff. But

102

there's one got something different. One you can't **hold**
back. That's the one you'll see at Olympia of a Christmas."

Nicky looked puzzled.

"Do you mean I play well?"

Annie sniffed.

"No. Anyhow, I've never seen you. Judging by the
trouble you take I should say you play like a foot. But
what I do say is that if you did work, and knew your stuff
backward, you got it in you to go right up. Trust me. I
know."

Nicky felt excited. Was Annie right? If she worked,
could she? If she worked! There was the point. She
thought work such a bore. Would she do it? She could.
Why not? Secretly, so that no one would know. It would
be nice if she was really good. Such a surprise for
everybody.

"I'd like to play well. Perhaps I'll try."

"I should." Annie looked at the clock. "No time like the
present. You take your racket. Pop along out and do a bit
of practicin'. When you've finished I'll have a cake for
you, hot from the oven."

Nicky had been the black sheep for so long she simply
could not start being a white one. No one knew but Annie
how hard she worked. If anybody came out she would lie
down on her racket and pretend to be doing nothing. She
got a kind of pleasure at getting things right all by herself.
Of course, it was Annie who made her stick at it.

"Now then, where's all the tennis practicin' we heard so
much about?"

"Well, I thought—" Nicky would start to explain.

"Whatever you was thinkin' will keep," Annie would
retort. "You go out and swing that bat."

All the same, quarters of an hour practicing tennis,
walks with David and Agag, spending pennies with Mrs.

Pettigrew, and gossips with Annie did not make a very gay vacation. Nicky got crosser every day. Luckily for her something nice happened at the end of it.

One day after tea they had all been playing a game of cards, but Nicky was cross and David would talk to Agag, so they gave it up. Jim lay flat on his back and stared at the ceiling.

"I wish we could go and see Annie's father's circus."

"One would have thought," said Nicky, "a boy who belonged to a tennis club, and who could go out alone, wouldn't have wanted any more."

"Oh, shut up!" Jim growled. "How you grumble! As a matter of fact, it was because of something I saw in a paper at our club. It was about a man in a circus who could walk on the ceiling like a fly, holding on upside down."

Susan sat beside him holding her knees.

"He couldn't really, could he? It must be some sort of trick."

Jim rolled over.

"There was a picture of him. I think it must be something in his boots."

"But flies don't wear boots," Nicky objected. "How do they keep up?"

Jim looked scornful.

"Suction, silly."

David was building a house out of the cards.

"I've some 'formation."

Nicky was drawing a picture on the window with spit.

"What do you mean?"

"The little fathead means he thinks he knows something," Jim explained; "but I bet he doesn't."

David carefully put another card on his house.

"I'm going to sing at a concert—"

104

"Stale news," Nicky interrupted.

"An' when I was practicin' with Pinny this mornin' Daddy came in and told Mummy somethin'."

"Well, what?" Jim asked. "Do get on."

David put another card onto his house.

"I only heard part because I was singin'."

Nicky turned around.

"Nobody wants to know about your singing. What did Daddy say?"

"I like talking about my singin'." David's house fell down. He carefully collected the cards and began re-building. "At the concert I'm going to sing *The Camel's Hump,* and Pinny says *Firs' Frien'* as an encore."

"You probably won't get an encore," Susan told him severely. "It's very conceited to think you will. Tell us what Daddy said."

David stopped building.

"He said he'd jus' seen Annie and she'd had a letter from her father. I didn't ac'ually hear what he said next. Then he said somethin' about tickets."

"Tickets!" They all spoke at once. They came and sat around David.

"Didn't you hear any more?"

"Do you think they were for us?"

"Do you think they were for Annie's father's circus?"

They were in the middle of trying to find out more when Mrs. Heath came in.

"Hello, darlings! Just a minute while I take off my hat and coat. I've got a surprise for you all."

Susan jumped up and put her arms around her mother's waist.

"Don't take off your things. Tell us now."

Nicky caught hold of her hand.

"Mummy, is it a circus?"

105

Mrs. Heath looked at the eight eyes staring up at her. Then she just looked at David.

"So you did hear. I wondered." She turned back to the others. "Yes, a circus. It's Annie's party. You're going to Southend to see it. Her father's invited you."

They had a most wonderful day at Southend. They went quite early and spent the morning on the beach. They paddled. They took with them a picnic lunch which they ate on the beach. They had it early because, although the circus did not begin until two, Annie wanted to get them up to the ground before, so that they could see something of the fair.

Susan stood gaping at all the stalls and merry-go-rounds. "Oh, Annie, it's lovely!"

"Ah, you should see it at night," said Annie. "Lit up. You're talking then."

They had only a few pennies with them. The most exciting things cost sixpence to do. Luckily Annie knew the man who had the merry-go-round. She must have known him well, because she called him Alf.

"Let's have a ride, Alf."

Alf proved to be an awfully nice man. He let them all ride. They each chose an animal. David a lion. Jim a horse. Susan an ostrich. Nicky rode on what she said was a rabbit. The others thought it was a sort of leopard.

After the first feeling of it being odd to keep going around had worn off, they enjoyed themselves tremendously. The organ in the middle screamed cheerful tunes. They screamed at each other. They had to scream or they could not hear. Just at first they waved at Annie and Alf each time they passed them. Then, as they went faster, they needed both hands to hold on and, anyhow, they were going so fast that Annie and Alf got blurred and looked almost like one person. Just as it seemed as if all the world were spinning, and if only they could spin a little faster they would go into a new world, the animals slowed down. Then they stopped. They got off very regretfully, if rather giddily. They found Annie and Alf.

"Oh, thank you," they all gasped. "It was lovely."

Alf grinned.

"Enjoyed it? Then why did you get off?"

"Do you mean"—Nicky caught hold of his hand—"that you'd let us ride again?"

"That's right. Scram. They've just started."

The second ride seemed almost better than the first. David expressed how they all felt when he said:

"I didn't feel I was me anymore."

The circus was quite perfect. There were all the things in it there ought to be at a circus. A very grand procession at the beginning. First the artists, then a whole collection of little dogs, who wore coats and trousers. Then the sea lions, three of them carrying balls on their noses. Then the horses, six grays, six chestnuts, and a little piebald pony pulling a cart. Then came a chimpanzee riding a bicycle. Last of all, the clowns.

All circuses are exciting, but your first is your best, because you do not compare it with anything. The Heaths sat right in the front with their mouths dropping open with excitement. All the circus people either knew Annie, or knew who she was. So when the clowns came into the ring they directed most of their tricks at the children. They threw balls at them. One, who was dressed as a cat, came and stroked Susan's face. Another one pretended he was going to throw a bucket of water at them, which made them all shrink back and the audience laugh. Nicky and David thought this the best part of the circus. They roared with laughter. David could not get over the goodness of the clowns in condescending to play with them.

"He throwed that ball at me, Annie, delibra'ly."

"Yes, dear," Annie agreed. "It's almost as if he's crazy to do a thing like that."

Jim and Susan did not care for the clowns. They would have liked them, but they thought it was dreadful, the rest of the audience looking at them.

"Annie, do tell the clowns to go away," Susan begged. "Everybody is looking at us."

"Well, it won't make them blind," said Annie. "We aren't doing anything we need be ashamed of, are we?"

From the twins' point of view Nicky brought more shame on them than the clowns. One of them, dressed as a baby, was pushed by another, dressed as a nurse, in what looked like a pram, around the edge of the ring. Just before they reached the children the nurse tripped, and the baby was thrown out. Quick as lightning Nicky was out of her seat and helping to pick him up.

"Goodness!" she said when she reached him. "You're a man!" She looked so surprised that the audience laughed. The clown took Nicky's hand and made her bow with him. Everybody clapped.

Jim and Susan attacked Nicky the moment she got back to her seat.

"What a show you made of yourself," Jim growled.

"Nicky, how could you," said Susan. "People must have thought it terribly queer."

"I don't see why they should," Nicky objected. "I thought he was a real baby. If he was, we'd have had to pick him up."

"You couldn't have thought him a real baby," Jim argued. "It was a man in a baby's bonnet. Any fool could see that."

Nicky grinned.

"Any fool, yes, but not Nicky Heath."

"But don't you see—" Susan broke in.

"Shh!" said Nicky. "Don't talk. Here come the sea lions."

The big moment for all of them was the appearance of Annie's father. Having always been used to Annie in a cap and apron, they were not prepared for the magnificence of her father. His face was perhaps rather lined, but a lot of pink and white paint hid it. The rest of him was very grand indeed. He wore pink tights all over, and with them silver-spangled shorts. On the program he was not put down as George Smith, which was his name, but as *The Great Godolphin, the Flying Wonder.* And in small letters underneath: *Assisted by Mademoiselle Leticia.*

Mademoiselle Leticia strained the children's allegiance to Annie. They had come to the circus convinced that if only she had both arms nobody would have been as good as she. But when Mademoiselle Leticia came in they wavered. She was small. She had golden hair and blue eyes. She, too, wore pink tights, but instead of the spangled shorts she wore fluffy pink skirts. David was the only one to express what they all felt. He said in tones of frank disbelief:

"Annie, did you ever look like that?"

Annie snorted contemptuously.

"And better. That's Lily Briggs. Known her since she was knee-high to a grasshopper. Her father was handyman with an elephant we once had. Sniffy, peaky little thing she was."

"Was she?" Susan tried not to sound too surprised. It looked as though she were doubting if Annie was speaking the truth.

While they were talking Annie's father and Mademoiselle Leticia climbed up swinging ladders onto trapezes hung from the roof. The band played a waltz.

Unless it is an old-fashioned turn, such as seeing a

109

ballerina jump off a horse's back through a paper hoop, there is no more beautiful act of the circus than trapeze work. Actually, Annie's father was nowhere near first-class. Most of what he did was done in a hundred other circuses all over the world.

Naturally, as it was their first circus, the children did not know this. They thought what they saw was marvelous. They could only gasp. Owing to their tennis training they had just sufficient knowledge to appreciate what perfection of timing and control of the body even the simplest movement meant. When at last the two figures climbed to the ground and bowed, they clapped till they were almost black in the face.

Because the children knew that before she had broken her arm, whether she looked as nice as Mademoiselle Leticia or not, Annie had actually done this act, they could never look upon her quite the same again. It was all very well for Annie to pull out a strand of toffee and show how a flying trapeze worked. Then it had all been part of a fairy story. Now they knew.

They met the Great Godolphin for a moment afterward. In the air he had seemed like a god. In a dressing gown he did not seem very important.

"Well, Annie, my girl," he said. "Got good seats, I saw."

"These are the Masters and Miss Heaths, Dad. This is Jim. Here's his twin, Susan. This is Nicky. This here's David."

Annie's father shook hands all around. Then he turned to Nicky.

"It was you that went to pick old George up. Thought he was a baby, didn't you? Said he laughed fit to bust."

Annie nodded. Then she gave her father a wink.

"We're not backward in coming forward. Not this one."

They had to go after that to catch the train back to

110

London. All the way up in the train they asked Annie about trapezes. How she learned. How much time she practiced. If she earned much money. Annie answered all the questions.

"It must have been a lovely life," said Susan enviously. "It does seem mean you have to live with us instead."

"Wonderful luck to have anywhere to live," Annie pointed out philosophically.

Jim sighed.

"It seems such a waste after all the training you've done."

"There never could be no waste in training," Annie said firmly. "Makes me handy in getting about even now."

David leaned against her.

"Annie, do you suppose that if he worked and worked Agag could be good enough for a circus?"

Annie laughed.

"I don't quite see him putting his back into it."

"I don't see why not," David objected. "He's got a lot of back."

Nicky half lay down, so that her feet would reach the seat opposite.

"I think I'd rather like to go into a circus."

"You'd be a fat lot of good," said Jim scornfully. "You'd never bother to learn anything."

"I wouldn't be so sure of that, Jim." Annie collected the lunch basket from the rack. "Many surprises in this world."

Annie saying this amazed the twins. They had no time to answer, though, for at that moment they came into Liverpool Street.

8

Acting "Cinderella"

The Christmas of that year Jim and Susan played in their club tournament. They had no chance, as it was open and drew first-class children from all over the country. It started on the Monday after Christmas and went on for a week. This, they thought, was a splendid week to have a tournament in, as it prevented that nothing-nice-will-ever-happen-again feeling on Christmas night. The twins entered for the singles and the mixed doubles.

The tennis tournament was not the only thing of importance happening that holiday. There was as well to be a play in aid of the hospital. They were all acting. It was *Cinderella,* and rehearsals began immediately after Christmas. The twins felt very important when they explained that during the tournament week they could not promise to come to rehearsals until after six o'clock. They spoke as if they expected to remain in for round after round. Actually, of course, they were not likely to get through one round.

Nicky was jealous about the tournament.

"It's mean, you know, all the things you two get. First the club, and now playing in the tournament. I don't ever seem to get anything at all."

"But you, will," Jim argued. "When I'm out working you'll still be lolling about at school and playing at the club. If it comes to that, it must seem very mean to David too. He's got longer to wait than you have."

David looked up from a new section of farm that he had for Christmas.

"I'm perfec'ly sa'sfied."

Nicky picked up one of his cows and turned it over.

"Then you shouldn't be. We haven't even got as good parts in the play as they have. I can't see why Susan had to be Cinderella as well as play in a tournament."

"Well, you couldn't expect to be it yourself," Jim pointed out. "You haven't got the hair for it."

Nicky looked sadly at Susan's braids. It was an odd world. What luck Susan had! Fancy being born with hair that made it perfectly certain that you would play Cinderella.

"As a matter of fact," Susan told her, "I think I would rather be the court jester. Besides, you're going to do juggling. People will think that awfully clever, not knowing about Annie."

"Ac'ually the best thing is me," said David. "I have two songs to sing."

Susan looked at him in despair.

"Isn't he awful? I don't know how anyone can be as conceited as you, David."

Nicky squatted down beside the farm. She rearranged a whole row of cows. Instead of waiting to be milked they now looked as if they were going to do a round dance.

"I'm not co'ceited," David explained. "I jus' can sing."

"Because you can do things," Jim said, "especially if it's things like singing, you don't want to slop about all over the place telling people about it."

"I don't slop. I just tell." David slapped Nicky's hand. "Will you leave those cows alone. I have to make my milk returns to the gov'nent. Moving them about upsets them."

"Don't be mean." Nicky helped to put the cows back in

113

their proper places. "I have to play with other people's presents from Daddy and Mummy, because I only get umbrellas."

"Well, whose fault is that?" Jim pointed out.

Nicky rolled over and picked up Agag's front paws and tried to teach him to dance.

"Mine. I never said it wasn't. Four umbrellas I've had. Next birthday I'm going to ask for something that nobody in the house likes but me, and I'll go and play with it by myself, because you've all been so nasty."

"We haven't," Susan objected. "I've got *Pride and Prejudice*. You wouldn't like that."

"And I had *Kim*," said Jim, "which you wouldn't understand."

"You never care nothin' for farmin'," David pointed out.

Agag, tried beyond endurance by being forced to dance on his two little back legs, gave a moan. Jim, Susan, and David were very indignant.

"Put him down, Nicky."

"It's a shame to tease him, poor little fellow."

"If I was him, I'd have bitten you; bein' him, he's too p'lite."

Nicky patted Agag.

"He doesn't mind a bit, do you, darling?"

Agag never was a dog to bear a grudge. He licked Nicky's face. He had no idea he was letting the others down.

"That dog," said David in disgust, "has too f'lict'us a nature."

Jim clicked his fingers to bring Agag over to him.

"Felicitous, you mean." He picked up Agag. "Have you got a felicitous nature, old boy?" Agag yawned. "He says he doesn't know what felicitous means, and he thinks long words for show are silly."

David, quite unmoved, went on arranging his farm.

"Agag and me un'erstan's each other."

Susan and Jim were both knocked out of the singles on the same morning. Susan did not play anything like as well as she could. She was unlucky in that she drew against one of the best players. She did not mind being knocked out by her, but she did dislike the gallery she collected. She felt sure everybody was saying what a bore it was for a good player to have to waste her time playing against her.

Jim played quite well. He had spent most of the summer term and the early part of the autumn term in training for swimming contests. He really showed signs of being quite exceptional. As soon as the swimming season was over he had done what he could to work at his tennis. He practiced against a wall whenever he got a chance, and played what squash he could. He took two games in one set, and one in the other, off a boy of sixteen.

Nicky came and watched them play in the doubles. Jim and Susan did what they could to prevent her being brought, but she pleaded to be allowed to watch, and Dr. Heath said, as long as she behaved herself, he could not see why not. Neither Jim nor Susan had the slightest hope that she would behave herself. She sat beside her father in the front of the gallery.

"Look at Nicky," said Susan gloomily to Jim, as they came onto the court. "I do hope she won't call out anything."

As a matter of fact Nicky behaved perfectly. She made no remark about the game at all. It was not a bad match. The twins were up against a pair very little older than themselves, and if Jim had been playing as well as he had

115

in the singles, they might have won. He was very anxious not to let Susan down and so went back to his old trick of attempting a killing service. Unfortunately he hardly ever got it over, and never the miserable little tap that followed as a second ball. He served fault after fault.

"I'm so sorry, Sukie," he whispered.

"Don't bother," she whispered back. "Why don't you do that other service? You got very good at that."

Even in the middle of the match Jim could not resist an argument.

"I can do this all right, really. I don't know what's wrong with it today."

Susan did not say anything more. She had to get ready to take a service. In any case, she never argued with Jim. It was a waste of time.

After the match was over they went to the changing rooms and had a shower, and then came up and joined their father and Nicky. Nicky looked up at them.

"Well tried, dears."

Jim could have hit her.

"Thank you. We don't want any criticism from you."

"A pity," said Nicky. "You should listen to Miss Nicky Heath. She could help you a lot."

"Oh, shut up, Nicky!" Susan whispered. She looked around anxiously to see if anyone could hear.

Dr. Heath pulled Susan down beside him.

"Not bad, old lady. On the whole I was pleased with you. You're becoming quite a stylist anyway."

Jim felt that this praise for Susan was really intended as a criticism of the way he had mucked up his service.

"That service of mine," he said truculently, "comes off nine times out of ten."

Nicky grinned.

"Sad it was ten all day today. Must be Christmas."

"Oh, shut up!"

"Yes, shut up, Nicky," Dr. Heath agreed. "Jim doesn't need you or anybody else to tell him he messed up his service. He knows it for himself."

Jim would have liked to argue. It was not altogether his fault. Even the best players found their service go wrong sometimes. But he felt he was beaten this time. It was true he had mucked the thing up. He was very sick with himself for doing it. Only there were days when it did come off. He could not help trying it just in case. It would be grand to serve like that in your club with everybody watching.

"Do you want to go," Dr. Heath asked, "or shall we watch for a bit?"

At the moment the game below finished and two more pairs came out. Susan looked down at them.

"Let's watch," she whispered. "They are supposed to be frightfully good. Someone told me that the two on the other side might win."

The game began. It was very fast. Jim and Susan watched in impressed, if now and again critical, silence. Nicky hung over the edge of the gallery, enormously interested. Suddenly she turned to her father.

"That girl"—she pointed at one of the players—"is very weak on her backhand, isn't she?"

Jim and Susan turned scarlet. They looked around to be sure no one was listening. They were afraid they might be asked to resign from the club if the people heard Nicky being so rude. Fortunately no one was within earshot. Dr. Heath pulled Nicky back into her seat.

"You've no right to criticize out loud like that. If any one is going to complain, it would be her partner."

"But she is weak on her backhand," Nicky argued.

"You said it was a thing that nobody who played well would ever be."

"Well, neither would they," her father whispered.

Nicky's voice grew louder as she argued.

"Do you mean those girls don't play well?" she said clearly.

Jim and Susan were in agony. Jim pinched Nicky's arm.

"Do shut up, Nicky. I'm sure they can hear. You might think of us. We shall look awful."

"Well, I want to know." Nicky's voice was louder than ever. "If good players are good at backhands and that girl isn't good at backhands, then she isn't a good player, and Susan said she was."

Susan looked imploringly at her father.

"Do make her stop. I'm sure they can hear."

Dr. Heath turned to Nicky. He spoke very severely.

"One more word, and you'll go out and sit in the car until we are ready to go home."

Nicky closed her lips tight. She thought they were all against her as usual. She leaned forward to watch the game, but she had the parting word.

"She doesn't play well," she hissed at the twins.

Because of Nicky's bad behavior she was not allowed to come and watch the finals on Saturday. She was very angry, because she enjoyed watching tennis. Besides, she considered that she had been right. Anyway, she had a perfect right to criticize. She thought it most unfair that she should be punished.

The twins went with their father and enjoyed every minute of the games. The day was made particularly exciting for Susan. They were sitting watching when Dr. Heath was tapped on the shoulder. He looked around. It was a man who wrote about tennis for one of the papers. He had been at Cambridge with Dr. Heath.

"Thomas Heath, isn't it?" he said. Dr. Heath nodded. The man looked at Jim and Susan. "I had no idea this couple of redheads were yours."

"I've two more even redder at home."

The man pulled one of Susan's braids.

"How old is this lady?"

"Eleven and a half."

The man turned to Susan.

"You like the game, don't you? I saw you play your singles." He looked back again at Dr. Heath. "I rather think you've a chip off the old block here. My word, you were a tiger at the game." He nodded at Susan. "You ought to have her coached."

Dr. Heath sighed.

"I've rather a large family. I'm coaching them all myself at present. Later on I think their grandfather means to give them some lessons."

"Good." The man got up. "Well, I must go and make some notes for my paper. Hope to see some of your redheads at Wimbledon in the future. Feel quite hopeful about this lady."

When he had gone Dr. Heath smiled at Susan.

"How's that, Sukey? That's Jeffrey Miller. He writes about tennis. He is supposed to be one of the greatest experts living. You heard him say that he thought you were promising. That's a lot from him."

Susan was so pleased that she had a lump in her throat. She did not answer. She just gave her father a look which she knew he knew meant that she was most awfully pleased. The only flaw in being praised like that was that Jim was left out. She did wish it was the doubles that Mr. Miller had seen, then they would have been praised together, which would have been so much nicer.

It was a good thing for the twins that they had the play

119

rehearsals to go to for the rest of the vacation, because otherwise they would have felt flat after the tournament was over. *Cinderella* was a grand performance in a hall that had proper lighting. Footlights, and battens of lights overhead, and spotlights to throw on people. Best of all, the lights changed color, so that really fine effects could be got.

Susan was not honestly a very good actress. She moved beautifully in the ordinary way, but she got awkward on the stage. Of course, with rehearsals, she got used to people watching and she knew it would be easier when she was dressed up, but all the same she was a little angular.

Jim was the prince. He was rather good. He enjoyed the whole thing, except dancing in the minuet at the Court ball.

Nicky was one of the people brought in as extras at the Court ball. She was the jester. She had a lot of knocking people over the head with balloons to do. As well, she did her juggling with two balls. Annie worked very hard to teach her to use three before the first night. It was no good. She always dropped the third ball. So she had to go on using two. She thought it looked more clever to have two balls that were always in the air than use three when one was likely to be on the floor.

David was the page who brought around the shoe the morning after the ball. He had a better part than that sounds because of his songs. There were not any songs in his part really, but two were put in. He sang *Cherry Ripe* in one act and *Matthew, Mark, Luke, and John* in the other. They were not really very suitable songs for a page, but they were songs which he could sing well, and everybody thought that more important.

Everybody came to see the play, including Grandfather,

120

who came to stay especially for it. It was a night of triumph for them all. Actually the most successful people were the ugly sisters and the two men who made up a horse, and, of course, the Heaths were not lucky enough to get those parts. But everybody was very proud of them.

Susan looked quite lovely as Cinderella. She wore brown rags at the beginning, which suited her long red hair. In the ballroom scene they had borrowed a ballet dress for her. It was the long kind that came down to the ankles. It was an easy dress for a transformation scene. A lot of fairies came on with the fairy godmother and they danced in front of her, hiding her from the audience, while the fairy godmother buttoned her up. She looked so nice in her ballet dress that when the fairies moved away, and the audience saw her, there was a burst of applause.

Jim was a surprise to everybody. He was a quite nice-looking boy, but nobody had thought very much about his face. Now, as Prince Charming, in a satin suit and a white wig, he looked really handsome. Everybody said: "How good-looking those Heath twins are," which made Dr. and Mrs. Heath feel very proud.

Nicky's odd-looking face was suited to her jester dress. She looked very small, and when she juggled with her two balls she got a tremendous round of applause.

One of the successes of the evening was David. He got an encore for both his songs. He was almost as popular as the ugly sisters and the two halves of the horse, and that was saying a great deal. The worst of David was that he was not at all surprised. He expected an encore, and would have been very hurt if he had not got it.

After the play was over somebody came on the stage and said that a hundred and twenty-three pounds had been made for the hospital, which was very good indeed.

121

When they got home Grandfather gave them each a wristwatch, because they had done so well. It really was a most exciting evening.

The next night, so that they would not feel too depressed, Grandfather took them all to see the pantomime of *Cinderella*. They had seats in the front row of the dress circle. It, too, was a very nice evening. Taking the matter all round, they thought that their performance of *Cinderella* was the better of the two.

"We did stick much more to the story," said Susan in the first intermission.

"You looked much prettier than that lady," David observed.

Grandfather opened a box of chocolates.

"I must say I preferred Susan meself."

"I can't think why they have to have that big fat girl for Prince Charming," Nicky complained. "I suppose at Christmas all the men actors are busy, so that they had to dress her up and pretend."

They were most surprised by the time they reached the next intermission. They had never been to a pantomime before, because they had missed the one they had meant to go to, by having measles. They never knew that in pantomimes it is the custom to dash about all over the world. So they were very startled when Cinderella, the two ugly sisters, and Cinderella's mother, who was dressed as an old lady with elastic-sided shoes, all came to stay at a smart hotel in Mars. Everybody went to Mars in balloons. There was a very funny scene in a balloon and a very exciting one, of rows of balloons flying across the backcloth. All the same, nobody felt that Mars was the right place for Cinderella to be in. They had to admit that the transformation scene was better done. There were twelve real ponies and a gold coach and proper coachmen, though

122

even then they thought Susan would look much nicer inside the coach than the other Cinderella. The end of the play was better than theirs. All the people that had been to the court ball came marching down a silver staircase. Jim hardly noticed the end of the play, because he was wondering so hard if it was possible to put up a staircase like that in their theater for next Christmas. They drove home quite dazed with so much dancing and singing and lights.

"Thank you so much, Grandfather," said Susan. "It was lovely."

"Yes, it was," Jim agreed. "Though I think they ought to stick more to the story."

"Don't you think, Grandfather"—Nicky snuggled against him—"there ought to have been a jester in the court scene, like me?"

David leaned against Grandfather's other side.

"It was all mos' sumt'us," he murmured, and went to sleep.

9

The Summer Term

Susan and Nicky shared a bedroom. It was not altogether a successful sort of sharing, as they had entirely different ideas about the things which ought to be in bedrooms. They made it fair by dividing the room in half. Each put what she liked (within reason) in her own half.

Susan, as the eldest, had the window end. This was nice. It had broad ledges to stand things on. Nicky had the half with the door. In Susan's half was the dressing table and the wardrobe. In Nicky's the chest of drawers and the armchair. As Nicky had no window ledges she had the top of the chest of drawers for putting things on. In both halves there was a bookshelf for their own books.

They had owned the room since they were small, so it had changed a lot as they grew older. There had been a time when Susan's window ledge had three teddy bears, a rabbit, and a golliwog on it. Now that she was almost twelve she had put those away, though, as a matter of fact, they were only in a drawer and she often took them out. Her window ledge now had quite a grown-up look. There was, of course, the clock she had won as a prize. Usually something was growing, bulbs in the winter, or a geranium during the rest of the year. There were framed pictures of tennis stars: they were not very good pictures, as they were mostly cut out of papers, but they gave a sporting look and went well with her prize clock. The middle of the window ledge she left clear. She never said why, and nobody but Jim knew that it was the space for the cups she hoped someday to win.

Nicky's end was usually in a bit of a mess. She had eleven animals. Most of them she had been so fond of she had worn holes in them. Pinny had done what she could with patches. But, of course, patched animals do not add to the smartness of a room. As well, when they could be had, she kept caterpillars. They lived in cardboard boxes with muslin over them, and though she cleaned them a lot, they never looked very spotless. At one time she had kept silkworms, but they had escaped and got into the beds. Unless you have found a silkworm in your bed you have no idea how nasty it is. It even put Nicky off, and, as she said, they never made silk anyway, and she did not know anybody with a mulberry tree, so they were sent back to the girl who had given them to her. She also kept a collection of musical instruments. She said it was nice to have something handy to make a noise with if she wanted to. There was a drum and a trumpet and a lot of squeakers and whistles out of snappers, and two music boxes from Woolworth's. Susan was used to Nicky and her noises, but she kept hoping she would get to like something else. She never said so, because she knew if she did, Nicky would find something noisier than ever.

As a matter of fact, Susan and Nicky got on better when they were in their beds than at any other time. Both going to St. Clair's, there was a lot to gossip about; and lying in bed, nothing else to do. As a rule they did not talk much at night because Nicky went to bed an hour earlier than Susan. But one night Susan went to bed early because she had a cold. Of course they talked, and it was then Nicky got her idea about joining the tennis club.

125

"I wish"—Susan blew her nose—"I knew sobe of those peoble at by club. When Jim's away I've no one to play with."

Nicky sat up in bed and held her knees.

"If it was me, I'd just walk about and say: 'Here's Nicky Heath. Anyone like a game?' "

Susan snuffled.

"You bould," she said noisily. "You don't do that sorb of thi'g in clubs. You don't talk to anybody till they talk to you."

Nicky wriggled with annoyance.

"If everybody who goes to clubs says they can't speak to anybody until somebody speaks to them, nobody will ever speak, because there's nobody to begin."

Susan blew her nose again.

"Well, of course, there's the peoble who play fearfully well. They know eberybody. There's a girl called Robemary. She plays terribly well. She spoke to be once. We were in the changi'g room. She said: 'Foul crush, isn't there?' I thought it was awfully nice of her."

Nicky lay down. She gave a deep sigh. She could not understand the way Susan thought.

"If it was me, I wouldn't be pleased. I'd expect people to be pleased if it was me spoke to them."

Susan turned her back.

"I wouldn't wait for that. It'll neber habben."

"You don't know," Nicky argued. "Everybody's pleased to talk to me at school."

"Whob?" Susan was very scornful. "Just the liddle girls in your own class. And what a class! It loses marks and marks for the house. An' it's nearly always your fault. You should hear whad Alison says. St. Catherine's is boddom nearly ebery week. Hardly adybody in your grade does thi'gs to earn marks."

126

"Lucky for the school," Nicky said nastily, "they have Susan Heath. She may have a cold in her nose, poor girl, but she never loses any marks. She's so good she couldn't be gooder. Everybody says you'll play in the second six this summer. Think of all the marks you'll earn then."

Susan was in an awkward position. She ought to refuse to speak to Nicky after impertinence like that. But she did want to know who the "everybody" was who said she'd play in the second tennis six. She decided to overlook Nicky's rudeness. She sat up, resting on her elbow.

"Who said so?"

"All the school." Nicky leaned out of bed to pick up her monkey that had fallen onto the floor. "Anyway, think for yourself. 'Course you will. Who else is there? I shouldn't wonder if you were a reserve for the first. The tennis is awful enough."

Susan picked a clean tissue out from under her pillow.

"Not awful enough for that."

"I don't know." Nicky tucked her monkey in beside her. "If you want to know, I think it was very silly of you to start playing. You'll be captain one day, and that'll be a lot to be proud of. Me, I shan't ever play at school at all."

Susan was in the middle of a particularly violent blow and could not answer for a moment. When she did she stammered with indignation.

"Bud you bust. Thad's one of the reasons why you ought to work, so you'b get into a tennis forb. Think of your house. St. Catherine's would mind much less about you if you're playing in a team."

Nicky stroked her monkey.

"I don't want St. Catherine's to mind less about me. I hate the silly house and the silly rules. When I'm so old I simply have to move up, I shan't play tennis, and nobody can make me."

Susan sighed. It never was any good arguing with Nicky. Sometimes she wondered if she was wrong in the head. It seemed impossible that any ordinary child could be born with such terribly upside-down ideas.

"When Jim's away," she explained, tucking her back in and settling down for the night, "school tennis is the only court practice I ged. Don't talk, I'm going to sleeb."

Nicky scowled into the night. How infuriating people were who just finished conversations. No one person, she thought, ought to be allowed to. It ought to take both the people who were talking.

"Suppose I still want to talk?" Susan made no answer. She even stopped her nose sniffing. Nicky made a face. Then she hummed. Susan knew that humming trick of old. If she grumbled, Nicky would only hum louder. She pretended to be asleep and hoped she would not give herself away by sneezing. Nicky did not really want to hum, and if Susan was asleep and could not hear, there was not much point in going on. She felt annoyed, but she, too, tucked in her back and settled down.

Although she settled down, Nicky did not go to sleep at once. She stared at a star which showed through the crack in the curtains. Odd, she thought, if one could get to the stars. Perhaps they would be quite nice to live on. Thinking of stars made her think of Rosemary, who had spoken to Susan. Perhaps she would be a tennis star. Not so good a star as Susan meant to be, but still a star. Stupid, she thought, not to let her join the club. How could any child be a tennis star who hadn't a court to play on, only a silly old wall? It was then she had her idea. Susan had said that when Jim was away school tennis was the only court practice she got. Her father must hate that. He thought school tennis bad for your game. Wouldn't he think it better if she joined and could play with Susan?

128

Nicky rolled herself more tightly into the bedclothes to help her think. Grown-ups were very tiresome. They had an idea that if they'd once said no they ought to stick to it, which was, of course, idiotic. She had got no about the tennis club from her father and mother and even from Pinny. It was no good going to any of them again. Then suddenly she thought: Grandfather! He had not said no. She would write him a letter. She would write tomorrow. Pleased at having had so sensible an idea, she went to sleep.

She wrote to Grandfather during the middle-of-the-morning break at school:

Dear Grandfather,
    I thought what a long time it was since I wrote to you did Susan tell you about the man who writes about tenis who told her she was good it is a pity she can't play at her club in the term becos Jim is away she has nobody to play with I am savving and savving to get enough money to join myself so I can play with her please give my love to James and Hibbert I hope the horses are quite well love from Nicky.

Nicky had spent last week's pocket money, so she had not got tuppence-ha'penny. She did not want to ask anyone for a stamp, because she did not want them to know she had written to Grandfather. She decided to borrow from Annie. She went to her when she got home.

"Now then," said Annie briskly. "You know I don't want you hanging about the big top when I'm dishing up."

"Well, all I wanted," Nicky explained, "was to know if you could lend me a stamp. I'll pay you back on Saturday."

Annie drained the water off a cabbage. "What's the

matter with asking the doctor? You know you don't pay for your own stamps. Or, if the doctor's out, that Miss Pinn will have one. She has your father's stamps—you know that as well as I do without troubling me."

"Well, you see"—Nicky lifted the top off the vegetable dish to see if the potatoes were in their coats, or just done in the dull way—"it's a letter to Grandfather, and I didn't want to say I'd written it."

Annie knelt down and opened the oven door to take out the roast.

"What have you written to your grandfather about? No good messing about with me. You're up to no good or we shouldn't have this hush-hush about the stamp."

"Well, as a matter of fact"—Nicky went over to the stove and gave an extra stir to the gravy—"I just wrote to tell him how good Susan was at tennis, and what a pity it was she couldn't use her club when Jim was away."

"Trust you." Annie lifted the roast onto the table. "They ought to take you on as a freak. The human serpent, or see how she twists. All the same, I'll lend you the stamp, because you'll be under my feet a little bit less if your granddad joins you to the club. Put the letter on the dresser. I'll see to it. Now go up and wash. My dinner's coming over in two shakes. And mind you," she called after Nicky, "tuppence-ha'penny on Saturday morning, or I'll know the reason why."

The answer from Grandfather came two days later. Annie did not put it on the breakfast table. She gave it to Nicky afterward in the kitchen.

"Here's the answer from your granddad. Thought you wouldn't want everybody being nosy about it."

Nicky opened the letter:

My dear Nicky,

If there is one thing I dislike in a man, or in a woman, it is hinting. Had you written directly and asked for a guinea to join the tennis club, I should have sent it at once. As it is, I am sending it to your father this morning. I have not told him that you have written to me, and I suggest that you do not show him this letter. But, as a secret between you and me, this subscription is instead of a birthday present for your tenth birthday, or a present at Christmas. Remember in future to ask outright. People can always say no.

Your affectionate
Grandfather

Nicky showed the letter to Annie, who read it and laughed.

"There are no flies on that old gentleman. Quite right too. I hate a lot of 'intin' meself. Unlucky with your Christmases and birthdays, you are. If he had only thought he could have sent you a nice umbrella."

Next birthday was still a good long way off, and Christmas was not until after that, so Nicky did not mind very much about the presents. The great thing was, she was joining the club. Her father told her that evening.

"Your grandfather has sent a guinea so that you may be able to play at the club, as he thinks it's dull for Susan with Jim away. I think you're a bit young for it, old lady. But I shall let you go up with Susan every day after tea on two understandings. You must obey Susan absolutely walking there and back. And you are not to make a nuisance of yourself up there. If you don't keep the rules, you won't go inside the place for another year at least."

131

Nicky hopped happily on one foot.

"Good! I am glad. 'Course I won't make a nuisance of myself. Why should I?"

Her father laughed.

"You'd be surprised to find that your long-suffering family would say, to a man, 'Why shouldn't you?' All the same, perhaps this time you'll behave yourself." He gave her an affectionate pat on the tail. "Mind you do. I shall hate to stop you going to the place, but I shall if there's any trouble."

As a matter of fact, Nicky was angelic at the club. She knew that her father meant every word he had said. She might, and did, carry on heated arguments with Susan as they walked there and back, but she obeyed her all right when it came to crossings and things like that.

All through that term they played every single day except at the weekends. When vacation came it was expected Nicky would stay at home. After all, Jim and Susan always had played against each other. But not at all.

"You aren't going to the club, are you, Nicky?" her mother asked at breakfast the day after Jim was home. "Come for a walk with me, David, and Agag. The other two have a court booked."

"Thank you." Nicky helped herself casually to some marmalade. "I've an engagement. I'm playing too. I've a court booked."

Susan looked surprised.

"Who on earth with?"

"A girl called June. She's the same age as me. Nobody to play with during vacation. We're going to play every day."

"You'll have to make it the same time as we go up, then," Jim pointed out. "You can't go alone."

132

Mrs. Heath poured out some more coffee.

"We'll manage, Nicky. You fix your game, and if it doesn't fit in with the others, Pinny or I will take you."

Nicky turned red. She was so used to thinking everybody was against her that she found it muddling when they showed they were nothing of the sort.

For one week of Easter vacation the children, Mrs. Heath, and Pinny went to stay with Grandfather. They went there because he would not be able to have them in the summer, as he was going abroad. They enjoyed the week at Easter, but they could not help feeling a bit depressed to think they were not going in the summer. They were fond of Tulse Hill, but not in August. On the night before Jim went back to school their father told them a secret. For the whole summer vacation he had rented a bungalow at Pevensey Bay.

When something nice is going to happen it seems to make time go slower. The summer term was really very nice. Jim broke the school swimming record for the 220 yards, and he won the championship cup for the second year. He had one more summer term before he went to Marlborough. If he could win the cup next year, it would be his altogether. No boy had ever won it outright. He enjoyed cricket. He played in the second eleven. He got some odd tennis practice. All the same, when he thought of Pevensey the days seemed as if they would never end.

Susan played in the first pair of the school second tennis six, and in the first pair of the house six. She still liked being like everybody else, but now she was a bit more than part of St. Clair's. She was Susan Heath, who's awfully good at tennis. It was nice for her sort of person to be a success, but she knew it did not mean much. At home the school tennis was treated as if it were Ping-Pong, and she never mentioned it if she could help it. All the same, the summer term was the nicest for her, yet she wanted to hurry it through. What was any summer term worth compared with going to Pevensey?

Nicky had been moved up. She was moved up because she was too old for her grade, and she was not allowed to think it was for any other reason. In her new grade she had to work. Her teacher thought it was bad for people to be always at the bottom of the class, and anybody who was she worked with out of school hours to help them catch up. Nicky had no intention of doing a spot of work when lessons were over, so she pulled herself together and kept a place about five from the bottom. Except for having to work harder she loved the summer term. She liked lying on a rug with a lot of friends watching people play matches. She found the smell of the grass mixed with rug, and the sun on her head, made her extra funny. She liked being the center person who made everybody else laugh. All the same, she had hardly ever seen the sea. She wished it were August.

David was supposed to do lessons with Pinny, but he struck.

"It's not," he explained to his father, "that she's not com'etent. But it's not the life for a man."

"That's all very well," his father had said, "but school's expensive. I'll send you when you're eight."

Probably that would have been the end of that if Grandfather had not come to stay for two weeks on his way abroad. He found David in the garden brushing Agag.

"Hello!" he said.

"Hello!" David got up and shook hands. "Daddy and Mummy have gone to meet you."

Grandfather sat down in a deck chair.

"Came by an earlier train. How's the dog?"

"You shouldn't never call a dog jus' 'dog,'" David protested. Then he added politely: "He's very well, thank you." He brushed Agag's tail. "I'm a little bored myself."

"Are you?" Grandfather lit a cigarette. "Sorry to hear about that. Why?"

David sighed.

"Edchucation. I don't care about it."

Grandfather smiled.

"Neither did I. All the same you have to have it."

"But not," David explained, "female toition."

The red hairs on Grandfather's eyebrow stood out stiffly.

"Who's teaching you? Pinny?"

"Pinny," David agreed sadly.

"Ah!" Grandfather looked thoughtfully at the sky. David went on brushing Agag. You would have thought they had finished with the subject of education, but suddenly Grandfather said: "Care to go to Eastbourne next term to this fellow Partridge?"

David rolled Agag over to brush his underneath.

"I would. Daddy says when I'm eight. Pinny says I ought to go to a choir school, which won't cost Daddy anythin'."

Grandfather made spluttering noises.

"Choir school! Got up pretty. Singin' all day long. Rubbish! Never heard such nonsense. You'll go to Partridge in the autumn. Knock this music nonsense out of you."

David paid no attention to Grandfather's being annoyed. He did not know what it was all about. He just went on brushing. Presently Grandfather felt sorry he had been angry. He gave David sixpence.

David put on Agag's collar. They walked together to Mrs. Pettigrew's. David had an ice-cream cone and a pink cake. Agag had a biscuit. His was free. He found it on the floor. On the way back they went to the butcher's, and David bought him a bone. They usually shared an unexpected windfall.

Dr. and Mrs. Heath were sitting with Grandfather. Mrs. Heath called David.

"Darling, you don't really want to go away to a boarding school, do you? You needn't go for a long time."

David wriggled free from her arm as politely as possible.

"I want to go now," he said.

Grandfather nodded.

"He shall go next term. Choir school indeed!"

David and Agag lay down under a tree in the corner of the garden. Agag lay on his tummy and ate his bone. David lay on his back and ate his pink cake. Next term! And before next term there was Pevensey! He felt so pleased inside to think of all the exciting things that were going to happen that he rolled Agag over. Of course Agag made the most dreadful growls. David looked at him severely.

"One more growl an' you won't be took to Pevensey."

However long time may seem in passing, it does go at last. There came a morning when Pinny, Nicky, and David got into a train. One hour later Dr. and Mrs. Heath, the twins, Agag, and Annie got into the car. Everybody set their noses for the sea.

10

Pevensey Bay

Pevensey was a most satisfactory seaside place because it never stopped smelling of the sea, which the children felt it ought to do. Everything was different from everything at Tulse Hill. They had a sort of lawn, but instead of green grass there was some grayish stuff that looked as if salt were mixed with it. The wall of the bungalow garden was also a seawall keeping out the beach. Being right on the beach like that gave a very coastguard feeling. It was the least grand of places. Nobody dressed up and there was nothing you could wear that was too shabby. When the girls put on ordinary clean cotton dresses and the boys a tie, they felt quite embarrassingly overdressed. They never did dress like that except on Sundays or to drive to Eastbourne or Bexhill. Ordinarily they had shorts and a shirt or sweater, or, of course, bathing things.

Bathing at Pevensey was the least fussy of affairs. There were a few bathing huts, but most people dressed and undressed on the beach. The Heaths, of course, changed in the bungalow. There was a small lavatory by the front door. In there Annie made them all leave their bathing things and wash their feet before they put their big towels around them and went to their rooms.

"Don't want half the beach in the house, and that's a fact."

"No, indeed," Pinny agreed.

The children tried to make both Annie and Pinny go into the water, but they would not. Pinny said:

"Well, dears, I may be foolish, but I feel rather a figure of fun in a bathing suit."

Annie snorted.

"What! Get into water what I seen horses walkin' in? Not me."

Under the garden wall a father and son kept boats for hire—the *Princess Anne*, the *Betsy*, the *Rose*, and the *Queen of the Ocean*. When anybody hired one of the boats the father, whose name was Dan, and the son, whose name was Joe, laid boards down to the beach, put the boat on them, and pushed it into the sea. All the children helped push. It was difficult to know whether Dan and Joe liked being helped because they never said anything. If a customer came, they spoke to him and told him what a boat would cost, but that was the end of the conversation. Joe chalked a figure on a slate. Dan picked up the slate and looked at it. Then in absolute silence they lifted the boat onto the boards and began to push. It was the same when it got to the sea. They helped the passengers in without a word, pushed the boat off as if they were tired of the sight of it, and walked back up the beach without a word. Jim thought, though he never said so, Dan and Joe must be glad of help, as he had timed how long it took with them helping and how long without, and when they helped it saved part of a minute. In any case, whether Dan and Joe liked it or not, the children liked helping. Seeing the boat off, waiting to pull it in again, the tar smell of boat on their hands, it was all very sea-doggish.

It was Dr. Heath who found out that Dan and Joe could hear, even if they said very little. He planned to go fishing. He came down to the seawall after breakfast. He leaned over it with his pipe in his mouth. Dan and Joe had the *Betsy* upside down and were mending something.

" 'Morning," he called out cheerfully. Dan and Joe jerked their heads sideways and said nothing. "Can I hire a boat this afternoon and some lines? Taking those kids of mine fishing."

Dan looked at Joe. Then he made a chalk mark on the slate.

"Barty got bait?"

Joe spat.

"Might have." He jerked his head at Dr. Heath. "He's got a motor."

Dan nodded.

"Ah!" They both went on with their work. Apparently they thought they had given all the information that was necessary.

Dr. Heath was quite used to getting things out of patients who did not want to talk.

"Where does Barty hang out?"

Dan felt in his pocket for a nail.

"Two miles this side Cooden."

"Right." Dr. Heath nodded and went away. Presently he got out the car and went the two miles this side of Cooden. He found Barty, and came back with a newspaper parcel of worms.

After lunch Dr. and Mrs. Heath and the twins came down to the beach. That was when they found out what a lot Dan and Joe heard. The moment they arrived they lifted the *Princess Anne* onto the boards, pushed her down to the sea. On the bottom of the boat some fishing lines were lying. Dan looked at the parcel of bait. Then he looked at Joe.

"Barty had bait," he said. They walked back up the beach.

That was the first of lots of days when Dr. Heath took out a boat. He was never happier. He would sit all day with his line running through his fingers and his pipe hanging out of the side of his mouth.

Jim tried to like fishing, but after a bit there always came a moment when putting worms onto his line made him yawn. Then he would decide to rest. Then he would shut his eyes. When he opened them again, the fish, the worms, and the family were all a bit out of focus. Then he would yawn again. After a time Dr. Heath would notice him yawning and suggest pulling in.

Susan loved being out fishing, but she never wanted to go if Jim did not, so they generally both stayed behind, because, although Jim was never actually seasick, he looked as if he easily might be.

Nicky and David loved fishing. But they were maddening in a boat. They would jump up suddenly. They both were apt to stick their hooks into themselves or other people. They never were clever at putting on their bait. The result was that only one of them was allowed to go at a time. They took turns.

Mrs. Heath always went. She very seldom bothered to fish, but would sit at the end of the boat and look at the sea and the sky, and think how lovely it was to have nothing to do.

On other afternoons they went for picnics. Across the marshes to Herstmonceux or to Pevensey Castle, or to the woods round Hellingly. They tried to go to as many woods as they could, because Agag liked them so much. He liked the beach, too, but it did not agree with him very well, because he would eat starfish and then he was sick.

On the afternoons when there was a picnic they all went, including Annie and Pinny. Annie was a grand person to have at a picnic. Living as she had done all her

140

life in trailers, she was wonderful at making a fire. From the moment they came to a place to picnic, it was Annie who took command.

"Now, then, Doctor, some nice little dry sticks. A couple of bricks from you, Jim. Don't you bother to go messin' about, mum, let the men do it, I say. What are a lot of men for if they can't do the fetchin' an' carryin'? Now, one of you men, I want three strong sticks all of a height." Dr. Heath, Jim, and David would fly around getting her what she wanted. It was grand to see the way she bound three sticks together for a tripod. She was clever about the wind too. By merely licking her finger she knew which way to let the draft run under her fire. Being with Annie on a picnic you felt almost as though you were a gypsy.

Dr. Heath decided to enter the twins and Nicky for the South of England Junior Lawn Tennis Tournament. It was to be held at the Devonshire Park, Eastbourne, in September.

They needed to work. Three or four swims a day had thrown their eyes out. For three weeks none of them had looked at a racket. They had that sleepy sandy feeling you get from days spent on a beach. The Pevensey vacation (even with Grandfather helping) had cost money, so there could not be much hiring of courts. The first thing was to find a wall they could use. They found that about a mile inland. A farmer had a barn. Dr. Heath asked if he might coach the children against it. The farmer laughed.

"Doan't see why not, surely. Reckon that barn has stood come all weathers for three hundred year. Reckon children playin' ball woan't lay it now."

Tennis practice was not the only trouble about the tournament. The tennis house, in spite of three ten shillings from Pinny, odd coins from the children, and some extra fees Dr. Heath had received and put in, was in a poor way. So was Susan's racket. It is impossible to give any racket the hard work hers had stood up to all the term and expect it to be anything else. It had, of course, been restrung, and she had used an old one for wall practice. All the same, it was pretty nearly finished. Nicky's racket was not a great deal better. She had, of course, not played at school. In fact, her family found it rather surprising how worn it was. They did not know her and Annie's secret about the practice she put in. As new rackets were out of the question, it was decided Susan must share Jim's, and Nicky's should be sent to be restrung. If the worst happened and Jim and Susan had to play their matches at the same moment, Susan was to borrow Nicky's. Of course, if they all played at the same time, Susan must just do what she could with her own.

Once they had entered for the tournament they gave up bathing. Instead they started off directly after breakfast for the farm where the wall was and were coached hard by Dr. Heath. Two afternoons a week they drove to some inexpensive hard courts and hired one for an hour. Dr. Heath played with Nicky against the twins. It was hot work for Nicky. As her father could not get about, she never stopped running.

Annie, though approving of any amount of hard work for the tournament, would not let them spend all their time practicing.

"Now then, Doctor, don't let all this tennis make you forget the fish. You go out for a couple of hours and bring back two good dinners for us all." Then one day she said: "None of you need fix anything for this afternoon, nor for any afternoons till your tournament starts. Goin' blackberryin', we are. God didn't put all that lovely fruit to drop to waste on the ground. What we can't eat now I'll set for jam."

"Yes, indeed," Pinny agreed. "Waste not, want not."

After two days' picking, all the family began to flag. They were so badly scratched, it was agony to wash. The sight of Annie with the baskets produced groans all around.

"Oh, no, Annie! Not today!"

But Annie was standing for no nonsense of that sort.

"Right. Starve if you want to. But there's some as cares." She looked meaningly at Pinny. "Some as would work their fingers to the bone."

"You mean pick their fingers to the bone," Jim objected.

Annie held out a basket to him.

"Pick or work, it's the same thing. Come on."

Except on a fishing day Dr. and Mrs. Heath were made to come and pick too. They gave in gracefully. Dr. Heath would grin at the children and get up with a sigh.

"As Annie says, she and Pinny'll pick for us even if we don't. Can't let them do that."

There was even worse in store for them all. One morning they were waked by bangs on their doors at five o'clock.

"What is it, Annie?" Mrs. Heath asked anxiously, supposing it was fire at least.

"Mushrooms," Annie said. "Lashin's of 'em. Come on, everybody. Can't let good food rot in the fields. There's a cup of tea for you all downstairs."

"But, Annie—" Dr. Heath started.

"Don't 'But, Annie' me, sir," she retorted. "Food's food. Can't let a lot of gypsies get it."

Luckily for everybody Annie's gypsies, or somebody else, found her field. Quite suddenly there were no more mushrooms. To say they were glad is to give a very low idea of how they felt. They were sick enough of picking mushrooms, but they had got to loathe eating them. The day the mushrooms gave out there was stew for lunch. David turned his helping over with his fork. He looked up in triumph.

"An' never an ed'ble fungi," he said thankfully.

The Eastbourne tournament was the first the children had played in where grown-up people were playing at the same time. This was one reason why Dr. Heath was so keen they should play in it. As competitors they would be allowed to watch other matches. He said they had got to watch every match they could, as there was no end to what could be learned in watching good people play.

The children felt very grand walking in and out of the Devonshire Park with their badges on. Their father came with them each day, but he could not watch the matches on the center courts as they could. He had a season entrance, but it did not provide a seat.

Each morning while the tournament lasted they got to the Devonshire Park at ten o'clock sharp. First they went to the referee's office to sign the attendance sheet. Then they took up good places to watch the matches. They brought a picnic lunch with them each day and Dr. Heath drove them either onto the downs or to the beach to eat it. After lunch they came back as quickly as possible. They ran to the referee's office. They signed the attendance sheet. Then they watched matches until teatime. Sometimes they missed tea and went on watching until it was time to go home.

While they were watching they criticized the play to each other. Even Nicky was sufficiently awed by the grandeur of the players not to speak above a whisper. Jim was tremendously impressed by the service of one of the men.

"See that, Sukey? You look at his feet. I don't believe

it's hitting hard that makes the ball go like that. It's because, as he hits it, all his weight is behind it."

Susan studied the service. She nodded.

"It's very good, isn't it. I don't see why you shouldn't practice that. It's something the same as yours means to be in a sort of way, only he doesn't just follow through with his racket, but with all of him. If we get home in time, we'll get Daddy to take us to the farm and you can practice."

Nicky sat hunched up glaring at the ball. She played a game with herself. She pretended to be one of the players. She always chose the best. She would put herself into their place. When the ball came over the net she would decide to what place on the court she would have returned it. With the better players she was humiliated to find that they hardly ever agreed with her.

Nicky played her tournament first and no one saw her play it. Her father had gone out to fish. The twins were watching a most impressive singles. They heard Nicky's name called through the megaphone.

"Oh, I say, Nicky," Susan exclaimed. "Do you mind awfully if we don't come and watch? We do want to see the end of this."

Nicky got up.

"Miss Nicky Heath is quite able to play without assistance," she said proudly, and strutted off.

Nicky's opponent was a girl of fourteen. Perhaps Nicky had not practiced enough, or perhaps she missed having an audience, for no one was watching at all, but the girl beat her with the loss of only two games. Nicky came back and joined the others feeling very hangdog.

"Well, how did you do?" Jim asked.

Nicky looked proud.

145

"We were not at our best. In any case, I didn't care if I won or not."

Susan looked at her severely.

"Something awful will happen to you one day when you tell lies like that." Her voice changed to interest. "What was she like?"

"Fat." Nicky made a face. "With great big legs that looked awful in socks. She got wet when she got hot."

Jim was the next to play. They all watched his match. He put up a very good show except once more had trouble with his service. This time he was not trying to send a killing first ball, but he was trying the service he had admired on the center court. Naturally, as he had only practiced it for an odd half-hour or so, he was nowhere near mastering it. It was rather a pathetic effort. All the same, by the end of the match he had got some feel of what he wanted. He was only just beaten. His father gave him a lemonade.

"That service ought to suit you when you've got the hang of it. Stupid to try it out in a tournament, though. But it's shaping. When we get back you must go up to the club and get some practice. Might work at it during the term, when you get a chance. You could do some good if you go on as you are doing."

On the day when Susan was to play her first match an awful thing happened. Agag was lost.

As dogs go Agag had unusually set habits. Every morning when Annie came down she opened the front door for him and let him out. This early morning walk was no smell, sniff, and saunter. Briskly, like a businessman catching the eight forty, he would set off up the road. No one knew where he went, but in about an hour he came home. Obviously, in his mind, this morning walk was what a day in the office is to a man. He felt when it was

146

over he deserved his comforts. He would lie down in his basket with a sigh of exhaustion. He would roll over onto his back. He would wriggle his rug so that it completely covered him. Then he would sleep. Later in the morning he was willing to put in an appearance. He would go for a walk, if a walk were going. In the winter he would leave his basket for a seat by the fire. In the summer he would lie in the sun in the garden. At Pevensey, if nothing better offered, he would find a starfish and eat it. But no matter where he was or what he was doing, at the first note of Annie's "Whoop, whoop! Coming over!" he was in the house and sitting by the place where his lunch would be put. He was not allowed his lunch before the family, and if they were late he would look up at them in the most injured way, as if to say:

"Really, can't a poor tired businessman have his meals on time?"

When his dinner came he swallowed it at top speed. Then he would sit down. He would study his empty plate and think over what he had just eaten. If he considered that he had been treated meanly, he had invented his own way of complaining. He would pick his plate up in his mouth and run around the table. He would pause now and again to tap it on the floor to show not only that it was empty, but there had not been enough in it to begin with. Usually he was lucky. None of the children could resist him when he had his plate in his mouth. Mrs. Heath was tired of saying:

"Darlings, you'll ruin his figure!"

Dr. Heath always said:

"The dog has had more than enough. Don't want to make a lapdog of him."

In the evenings either he was supposed to sit on the floor, or he could go into his basket, which lived in what

147

was called the flower room, though really rubbish room would have been a better name. But Agag was not a dog to bow to the opinions of others. Night after night he would come into the living room and sit down just where he wanted his basket put. First he kept up a series of little whines. Then when these were not attended to, and they never were, he began to bark. Every night the same sort of conversation followed. Mrs. Heath said:

"Be quiet, Agag. Don't let's give in to him, Pinny. He must learn. If he wants to go to bed, he must do it in the proper place."

Then Dr. Heath would look up.

"Quiet, Agag. Lie down, old man."

"Do be quiet, dear," Pinny would say gently. "You're disturbing dear kind master and mistress, and you know the doctor's tired."

Agag cared for none of these remarks. Nicky and David were in bed, but the twins were there to support him. He would throw them a look out of the corner of his eye, as much as to say: "How long do you give them before they give in?" Sure enough, after a bit either Dr. or Mrs. Heath would say to either Jim or Susan:

"I suppose we'll have no peace if he doesn't have his basket. Better get it for him. But he is a bad dog. He ought to learn."

Even when his basket was fetched that was not the end. On the hottest of nights he expected to be entirely covered by a rug. Just tucking him in was nowhere near enough. He expected a great deal of trouble taken. If the rug was not exactly as he liked it, he would get out of bed again and bark until it was put straight.

"Really, Agag," Mrs. Heath would say, "it's much too hot for a rug. Don't be ridiculous. Don't give in to him, Susan."

Dr. Heath would look at Agag severely.

"What a lily that dog is! Most unhealthy. Rolled up in a rug on a night like this. Lie down, old man. Nobody is going to bother with you."

Pinny would look up from her knitting.

"Naughty, naughty boy. Silence is golden, you know."

But Agag paid not the slightest attention. He knew his Jim and Susan. In a minute one of them would be across. They would tuck him in. Pat his rug in the proper places. Show a nice respect for the way a tired dog expected to be treated.

Susan's tennis match was looked foward to by them all. She had a bye, and Dr. Heath had seen the girl play in the first round who was now drawn against her. On form Susan should win.

On the day of the match Agag trotted out as usual, looking as though he were catching a train, and disappeared, but this morning he did not come back. Susan's match had been posted to be played at ten o'clock. Breakfast was at half-past eight. It was almost over before they realized that Agag was missing. There was the most frightful hullabaloo. They ran up and down the beach, shouting; but not a bark, not a sound. Susan came to her father with the tears pouring down her cheeks.

"I can't play. The poor little fellow may be hurt or drowned."

"I shan't go and watch," Nicky sniffed. "I must stay here and hunt."

Dr. Heath was as worried as everybody else, but he did not believe in scratching matches for which one had entered to play. He took both Nicky and Susan by an arm each.

"We're all going in. And Susan's going to win. Directly the match is over we'll ring up. If Agag isn't back, we'll all

149

come and help hunt. Is that agreed?" He looked first at Jim, then at Nicky, and last of all at Susan.

Susan tried terribly hard to stop crying. But she was certain somewhere a long little brown body was lying. Never to bark again or carry a plate. Her father took her by the chin. He turned up her face.

"Well, old lady, let's see your courage."

Susan forced her face into what was almost a smile.

"All right," she said. "I'm ready. Let's go."

Pinny patted her on the back.

"There's a splendid girl. Be sure I shall look for our little man. Many hands make light work, you know."

Jim was already in the car. He looked out of the window.

"Agag won't be found with hands. You ought to say either eyes or voices." But he spoke in so dispirited a way that nobody argued with him. They were all too depressed.

David was appalled at the tragedy that had fallen on the house. Agag gone. Susan crying, so that she could not win her tennis match. Directly the car had disappeared he set off inland. "It's me must find him," he told himself firmly.

David walked for about half a mile, calling Agag all the way. It was not very likely that he would find him. It was sandy country without much in the way of a rabbit, and there were marshes and water. Then suddenly he came to a group of cottages. Behind the first cottage was a garbage can. Standing up, looking into the garbage can, was Agag.

"Agag!" said David in a very shocked voice, for when you have been certain that your dog has either been drowned or caught in a trap, it is humiliating to find him stealing things out of a garbage can. Agag evidently felt he had done the wrong thing. He put down his tail. He came over to David with his legs so bent that he did not seem to have any at all. He seemed merely creeping along like a snake.

"You are a bad boy." David took off his sandal. He held Agag by the collar and hit him hard three times. Then he put on his sandal again, took Agag in his arms, and kissed him. Agag, with a tongue smelling of garbage can, licked David's face. They had as big a reunion scene as though he had been lost for days instead of only about two hours. All the same David said to him affectionately:

"All this lickin' isn't going to make things right. Susan thinks you're lost and she won't win. You an' me have got to go to Eastbourne."

It was all very well to say that they must go to Eastbourne, but how were a dog and a boy with no money to get there? David stopped a man who was going by on a bicycle.

"Could you tell me the time?" he asked politely.

The man looked at his watch.

"Ten to ten."

"Could you tell me," David went on, "how I would get to Eastbourne from here?"

"Bus," said the man over his shoulder. He pedaled on a little farther. Then he looked back again. "Be along in about five minutes."

David puzzled, as he often had before, at the stupidity of grown-ups. Neither he nor Agag looked moneyed people, yet the moment you asked how to get anywhere you were told "bus," just as if buses did not cost anything. Stupid to go about talking to people just as though everybody had money in their pockets. He looked up the street. A truck was coming toward them. He picked up Agag and stepped forward and held out his hand. The truck stopped.

"Well," said the man. "What's up?"

"Were you going to Eastbourne?" David asked politely. "If so, would you take me and my dog?" He looked down at Agag. "He's a very safe dog. He never bites."

The man opened the little door beside him.

"Hop in."

It was nice riding in the truck. The man said that he was taking wood for building a house. David explained all about Agag being lost and the tennis tournament. The man said, well, the wood was for the old town anyhow, and it wouldn't be far out of his way to drop David at the Devonshire Park. He agreed with David that Susan was very unlikely to win if she was worried about Agag being lost.

"Why," he said, "my missus had a cat called Jane. She was off for three days. Shocking, it was. My missus never stopped crying. I seemed to have no heart for me work."

David pulled Agag more securely onto his knee.

"And did Jane come back all right?"

The man nodded.

"Walked in as cool as a cucumber, with never a by your leave or anything."

David tried to picture a cat looking like a cucumber.

"Yes," he agreed. "She must have looked terribly thin. Never having eaten anything for three days."

The man blew his horn in a scornful sort of way.

"Don't you believe it. Cats always falls on their feet. Three days or three weeks, it's all one to them. Come in looking as fat as I don't know what."

"Oh!" said David, puzzling why the man knew that Jane looked like a cucumber, when he did not know what she looked like. "I wonder where she went to."

"Ah!" The man spoke in the gloomy tones of one who fears the worst. "That's a thing we won't never know." He stopped the truck. "Well, here's the Devonshire Park."

152

David got out of the truck and stood Agag in the street.

"Thank you very much indeed for your kindness," he said politely. "Please remember me to Jane and your missus."

"I will," the man agreed. "Hope Susan wins." He started the truck again and drove off.

David and Agag went to the entrance to the Devonshire Park, and for the first time he realized a terrible thing. It cost money to get in. There was a turnstile gate and people walking through, and some had tickets and some paid, but nobody got in for nothing. After a time he noticed that the man who was taking the money did not ask some of the people for a ticket or money. They began to get a ticket out of their bag or pocket, but the man always nodded.

"That's all right, sir," or "madam," he said. "Nice morning."

Presently a car drove up with a lady dressed in purple inside. She was obviously the sort of lady that people did not look at the tickets of; the sort people saluted and said good morning to. David took Agag under his arm and got close behind the lady. She had a great deal of skirt. He caught hold of a little bit of it.

"Good morning, madam," said the park attendant. "Nice day, isn't it?"

"Very," the lady agreed in the grandest kind of voice, and pushed through. David kept to the side of her that was farthest from the man. He pushed through too. Even fastened to the lady in purple he would never have got in for nothing, but luckily the man was taking some money from somebody else and did not notice him.

Lawn tennis, like everything else in the world, needs all your concentration to do well at it. Susan tried to give her match all her concentration. She served well, making very

153

few faults. She took her returns properly, getting quickly into the right positions. She used her wits and kept the other girl moving. But there was just the edge off her play. There was a lack of strength in her drives, a lack of energy in her service. When they changed courts she kept thinking: "Perhaps he's turning over and over in the sea, like a bottle. Perhaps I won't see him anymore." Then her eyes would fill with tears.

The family did not help her much. It was obvious from their long, miserable faces nobody but Dr. Heath was thinking about the game, and he was only part of the time.

Her opponent won the first set 6–4, then she won the first five games in the second set. "Oh, dear, I am being a disappointment to Daddy," Susan thought; "but I can't help it. What's it matter if I win or not, if Agag's dead." It was her service. She picked up two balls. She raised her racket. Then she was startled by a noise through the wire fencing behind her. She looked around. A shiny wet little nose was stuck through the hole in the wire. One blue eye and one brown eye were staring at her. David was holding Agag. He was panting with excitement.

"He's found, Sukey, he's found. Now you must win!"

Susan felt all swollen inside, she was so happy. She slammed her service across the net. She won her service. She won the next game. She won that set. Then she took the third set. "Game, set, and match to Susan Heath," said the umpire. Susan shook her opponent by the hand. Then she raced around to David.

"Did you know, in the middle, he was found, Sukey?" Nicky asked.

Dr. Heath pulled her braids.

"Did she know! You're a bad girl. Even losing Agag oughtn't to put you off your game." Then he smiled at her. "But it was grand to see you win."

154

11

The Tennis Coach

Susan got through three rounds in the South of England Junior Tournament. She was mentioned in the local papers. In fact, she felt she was somebody. She came back to Tulse Hill accepted as the best player in the family.

Being a bit of a success gave her a temporary confidence. She did very well indeed in the Junior Covered Court Championship at Christmas. She was not knocked out until the third round, and then it was by that year's champion. She might have had luck. The first girl she played against had a heavy cold. The second was weak anyway. She was only in the second round thanks to a bye. But still, Susan was not knocked out until the third round, which was something to be proud of.

For her match with the champion there was quite a gallery. Other players, other players' parents, critics from the newspapers. Susan hated all the staring faces, but she was getting more used to them. Besides, it gives you confidence to know you play fairly well, or at any rate are not likely to make a fool of yourself.

After the match several of the papers had things about her in them. They said Miss S. Heath had done very well to take two games off so experienced a player; they said her volleying was resolute. They said she made one or two splendid drop shots; they said she was apt to forget where her opponents' weaknesses lay, but she would remember with more experience; they said little Miss S. Heath had no chance against the brilliance of her adversary; she had, however, style and some good strokes when she got a chance to bring them off. In fact, they were very kind to her. Some of the picture papers had photographs of her. She was growing prettier as she grew up, and she really looked very nice in them. Even her family said she did not look bad, which was quite a compliment for them.

In the summer term she played in the school first six. They hardly ever won a match. The standard of tennis at St. Clair's certainly was not improving. On the other hand, nobody else on the team was only thirteen. The rest of the school thought her wonderful. Although she knew she was not, it was nice so many people thought so.

Jim had done well with Susan in the doubles of the Junior Hard Court Championship at Christmas. They got through a couple of rounds together. He thought he was lucky to have Susan to play with. He told her so one evening. They were cooking chestnuts.

"You know, Sukey, if you could find somebody better for next year, I wish you would. I don't get so much practice as you, and even if I did I wouldn't be as good. I don't get much chance at school. I don't suppose I'll get any at Marlborough."

Susan told him not to be an idiot.

"You would be just as good as me if you got more time at it."

Jim hesitated.

"You know, of course, Dad's frightfully keen on tennis, and so's Grandfather, but really I'm much keener on swimming. The sergeant told me that he believed I might

156

do some good at a longer distance presently. He thinks the 880 might be my mark."

Susan dug a knitting needle into another chestnut. She put it on the bars of the grate.

"Do you think they think that you could be really good? I mean break records, and Olympic Games and things like that?"

Jim pushed a chestnut off the fire. He squeezed it in his handkerchief to see if it was done.

"Oh, I don't know about that. You have to be frightfully good for that sort of thing. But I suppose I shall have a dab at anything that's going."

Susan eyed his chestnut.

"Is it done?" He shook his head. She took it from him and put it back on the bars. "Do you mean you would like to drop tennis altogether?"

"No." Jim wriggled. He tried to think of words to explain what he did mean. "But I shan't be first-class. As a matter of fact, I don't want to be. I'd like to be just good enough to get fun out of tournaments and things; be able to enter for the same things as you, but not hope to do anything at them."

Susan twisted a chestnut around, so that its other side was turned to the fire.

"Have you told Dad?"

Jim picked up Agag, who was asleep by the fire. He held him up in the air.

"I think he knows. I mean, you know what lots of things people do know without anything being said."

A chestnut popped. Susan picked it out of the fireplace. She squeezed it on the underside of her skirt.

"I don't suppose, anyway, he cares a bit what we're good at as long as we're good at something. He told me once he thought tennis was the most likely in our family.

157

But I expect he'll be just as pleased if it's swimming or skating or anything else. The awful thing is if none of us are every really good at anything."

Jim held out his hand for half the chestnut. He broke off a little bit and put it down to cool for Agag.

"You're doing your best, getting to be more of a star every minute."

Susan looked pleased.

"You'll be all right if you're a swimming champion. Goodness knows what Nicky and David will do."

Jim patted Agag.

"You're as fine a dog as anyone could imagine, aren't you?"

Susan leaned over and looked closely at the chestnuts.

"I believe they're all cooked."

Nicky had not done at all well in the Junior Hard Court Championship that Christmas. She was going through a difficult time. She had got the clearest picture in her mind of where every ball ought to go. How every stroke ought to look. Yet it was all coming out wrong. Annie was her comforter.

"You keep on at your practicing and don't mind. You're only eleven. Plenty of time yet."

"Did you do trapeze work when you were eleven?"

Annie laughed.

"Me! Bless you, yes. I was up on the trapeze time I was eight. 'Course it wasn't allowed, not by law it wasn't; but I was a big girl, and we generally had somebody's birth certificate handy if there was a rozzer along."

Nicky had talked too much with Annie not to know by now that a policeman, in the circus world, is called a rozzer.

"But where you good at eleven?"

Annie looked back over the years.

158

"Not to say good. Smart little nipper I was. We didn't do nothing very showy. Always worked with a net. Matter of fact I've a fancy that when I was about your age my dad started taking a stick to me. I tried doing a lot of things I couldn't. 'Fraid I'd break my neck, he was."

Nicky made a pattern with her finger in a bowl of flour that was on the kitchen table.

"But, Annie, I'm not trying to do anything I can't. I'm doing exactly the things Daddy taught me, and they're all coming out wrong."

Annie gave her hand a smack.

"Take your finger out of my flour. I wasn't never a you, and that's a fact."

Nicky screwed up her face.

"What's that mean?"

Annie jerked her head toward the door.

"It means that them as asks no questions won't be told no lies. You take your racket and go out and practice on that wall."

David loved being at school. He was at once put in the choir. By Christmas he was singing in the school concert. That Christmas there was enough in the tennis house to get him the racket that was owed him. His father began coaching him. As a matter of fact, while lying about the garden or playing with Agag, David had taken a very intelligent interest in what the others had been taught. He knew quite a lot before he started.

That summer Grandfather did not go abroad, so they all stayed with him as usual. Of course, it was awfully nice staying with Grandfather, but it was not Pevensey, and there was no getting away from it. Dr. Heath took the twins down a couple of days before the others. He had entered Susan for the Bournemouth Lawn Tennis Tournament. It was an open event. It was obvious that she could not do any good in it, but once more, first-class players were entered. It was a grand chance for her to see some decent play.

They drove over to Bournemouth three days running. Susan had a bye and was not knocked out until the third day. They were the most lovely three days. Apart from the tennis, which was good, they enjoyed picnicking on the beach, or in the country around. The whole place smelled of pine needles. It was the beginning of vacation. The sun shone every day.

"It's a pity," Susan said, "you can't keep nice things and put them away in a box."

Dr. Heath laughed.

"On a dirty, foggy night in November we'd say: 'Let's take out Bournemouth and sit among the pine trees for a bit.' "

"That's what I do mean," Susan agreed. "It would be nice if we could."

That summer there was another junior tournament in aid of charity. This year Susan won it and came home with a silver cup. Jim got the second boys' prize: a traveling clock.

Nicky did not play in the tournament. Two days before it she climbed up a plum tree to get some plums. The rule at Grandfather's about fruit was that finding was keeping, if it was on the ground. Nicky was obviously not looking on the ground. She fell off the tree and sprained her wrist. She tried to say nothing about it, because no one had seen her fall. She hoped her wrist would hurt less in a minute. But the minutes went by and, instead of hurting less, it hurt more and more, and turned blue and swelled up as though a bee had stung it. At last she could not bear it any longer and went to look for her father to have something done about it. He was sitting on the edge of the tennis court, watching Jim and Susan play. She set off toward him. The odd thing was, the nearer she got to him the farther off he seemed to go, and the fainter he became. She went on trying to get to him, but somehow she did not seem to manage it. David and Agag were playing with a ball. David happened to look up and he saw Nicky.

"My goo'ness," he said. "You look most peculiar."

Nicky did more than look peculiar, for at that moment she fell down in a faint.

As a matter of fact, when Nicky recovered she rather enjoyed her sprain. To begin with, she felt grand with her arm in a sling, and all the others were terribly interested in her faint.

"Do you mean to say," Susan asked, "that you were just walking along ordinarily and quite suddenly you didn't know anything anymore?"

"I didn't know anything," Nicky agreed proudly, "until I was on the sofa with my hand being tied up."

"But you must have dreamed," Jim argued. "There was a boy at school fainted once. He was quite different. He said he heard bells first. He was only unconscious for a minute, then he was as sick as anything all over the floor."

"It was a very good thing Nicky wasn't that," David put in, "because both me and Agag were sitting on the floor beside her while Daddy tied her up."

"I had real brandy to drink," Nicky said proudly. "I never even felt sick."

Her grandfather gave her a large basket of plums.

"I understand that you injured your wrist because you wanted these. Stupid to go climbing unless you know how to hold on. However, chew them up and get well soon."

When it came to the day of the tournament Nicky felt

low about her arm. It was all very well to look interesting with a sling, but it was much more interesting to be the other three with their tennis rackets, all wondering whom they would play against. However, she succeeded in having the sort of day she liked, the grown-ups making a fuss over her. Besides, one of the players said something which made her look on the whole family differently. It was a girl who had been asking about her arm. She said:

"Oh, well, it's a good thing one of you redheaded champions can't play."

Redheaded champions, indeed! Did people think of them like that?

Before they went home, Grandfather said he was arranging to have the whole lot of them coached. He told them about it one evening. The red whiskers were sticking out of his left eyebrow. They glinted in the light from his reading lamp.

"I understand the coach up at the tennis club is just about first-class. I'm fixing to have the lot of you have twelve lessons lastin' half an hour. An hour's too long. None of you could concentrate. I'm gettin' your father to sound this coachin' fellow as to how you're all shaping up. I'm keeping your coaching, David, until a year from this autumn. No good starting too young. You'll have two of your lessons at the end of this vacation, Jim, and the rest at Christmas or Easter. Susan, and Nicky if she doesn't go falling off more trees, can have two lessons a week, startin' when they get home."

Being coached professionally ought to have been fun. Jim wasted a good deal of his first two lessons arguing. About the only thing the coach found faultless was his racket. He said the weight was right and it was a good make. For the rest, he had a lot of improvements to suggest.

162

The coaching was begun by playing a game or two. During it weaknesses were spotted and worked at afterward. Inside him Jim knew they honestly were weaknesses. He knew he had always had them. They were exactly the same as his father had complained of from the beginning. On the other hand, he had just won a clock in a tournament. He belonged to a family who were supposed to be some good at the game. He was not a child to be ordered about. Wasn't he just going to a public school? He would never have admitted it, but inside he had expected the coach to be pretty flattering. When, at the end of two games, instead he heard a long list of things that were wrong, he simply had to argue.

The coach was absolutely unmoved by arguing. He knew Dr. Heath. He admired the way the family had been grounded and was determined to get everything into them he could. He grinned at Jim.

"All right," he agreed. "I'm all wrong. But you're here to be taught by me, and you've got to learn my way."

Susan, of course, slaved at her lessons. If she was disappointed at finding how much was wrong with her game she never showed it. Without a murmur she relearned many things from the beginning. She enjoyed every moment of her lessons. So did the coach. It is obviously more fun teaching people who are keen.

Nicky might have wasted her time as Jim did, in argument, if she had not had a conversation with Annie before her first lesson. Annie beckoned her into the kitchen, and dug her elbow into her in a knowing sort of way.

"This gentleman what you're havin' lessons from this afternoon. You pick up what you can. From all I hear, he's a real champ. There was a champ I saw once in a cat act. Wonderful he was. Walk in and out of the cage

163

among those great roaring beasts like as though they were so many mice."

"Was he afraid?"

"Couldn't say. Never saw him above once. Well, in our circus there was a Miss Umbopo and 'er dad. Mabel Lee her name was really. Gypsies, they was. They were traveling with one mangy old cat. I says to her: 'Mabel, there's a proper champ with the cats playing in that posh circus. You go and have a word with him. See if you can't pick up a tip or two.' Well, she says she'll go. But does she? No. About three weeks later her dad gets influenza and Mabel has to do the act with the old cat. In she walks, bold as brass. But the cat turns nasty. Before anything can be done he makes a spring at her."

"Goodness!" said Nicky. "What happened to Mabel?"

"Oh, she was corpsed." Annie spoke casually. "I sent a lovely wreath to the funeral. But even when I was paying for it, I said to myself: 'Annie,' I said, 'you wouldn't be paying for this now if Mabel had gone and learned from the champ.' "

Nicky pulled up her socks.

"I don't see what's going to eat me, even if I don't learn."

"Nothing will," said Annie darkly. "But you just fix your mind on Mabel."

Whether Nicky fixed her mind on Mabel or not, she certainly did work at her lessons. The coach was very good to her. He often gave her an extra five minutes or so. He started her exactly as he started the others. Only in her case, when he had seen her play, it seemed as though there was everything wrong everywhere. He started her off from the beginning. Her stance, her service, her forehand drive, her backhand drive, volleying, net play, lobs, and smashes. Then at last, right at the end of her

164

course of lessons, court tactics. He was very generous to her over these. He taught her a lot during her lessons, but still more in the talks he had with her outside her classes.

"Don't you forget that, though, of course, you've got to have a racket, and you've got to have a ball, and your body's got to be the right way around, and the arm that holds the racket has got to strike the ball, in the end it's the way you think that matters. You must think of every match you play as one person's brain against another's. I can give you, and other people can give you, all the strokes. You can have a natural gift, but it's all wasted until your brain is just that much better than your opponent's. No matter how good a stroke may be, it's only worth half if it isn't used cleverly."

Nicky nodded. They were sitting together in the gallery, waiting for a court.

"You mean, in the end you could stop thinking if you were doing things right or wrong, or whether you were standing right, but you couldn't ever stop thinking how best to win."

"It's exactly what I do mean." He looked at her in rather a puzzled way. "How old are you?"

"Eleven." Nicky gripped one of her knees with her arm and rested her chin on it. "I've had a very troubled life. Do you know, my twelfth birthday will be one of the only birthdays I ever had when I could have all my presents. First I had umbrellas and umbrellas. Then, when I joined this, it was part of Grandfather's birthday present and one Christmas too."

"Why did you have umbrellas?" he asked.

Nicky told the story of the umbrella man. He was interested to hear about the tennis house.

Nicky lolled back.

165

"It's not so bad just now. There's quite a lot of money in it. That's because Pinny keeps knitting jumpers, then Mummy had a little windfall over something that she thought would never pay again and did. Then Daddy had a few bad debts paid up. But it wouldn't have anything in it at all, if it wasn't for Grandfather. He's giving us you, and he is giving us all our subscriptions to the club for Christmas presents. The house has to get all the extra things, tennis rackets, balls, and entrance fees for the tournaments."

He nodded sympathetically.

"Bit of a struggle, I should think. Still, maybe in the end it will be worthwhile."

At that moment the court below was empty.

"There's our court," said Nicky. "I hope to be worthwhile, and Susan's sure to be. Come on!"

That Christmas only Jim and Susan entered for the Junior Hard Court Championship. Nicky and David had a piece of disgusting bad luck. They went to a party two days before Christmas, and soon afterward a child who had been at it came out with chicken pox.

Nicky stamped with rage.

"Quarantine for Christmas! I can't play in the tournament. Oh, it is mean!"

"It isn't even as if it was an exceptionally good party," David pointed out. "Life is most outrageous."

As a matter of fact, neither of them got chicken pox. Their grandfather sent them seats for the circus to make up for the quarantine. He also sent them five shillings each to spend on sideshows.

Pinny took them. She had a most miserable afternoon. She was afraid to let them go on the sideshows alone for fear she would lose them, so she joined them on scenic railways and whips and ghost trains and grew greener

166

and greener. In the end they had to take her to a pharma-
cist and give her sal volatile. Nicky and David enjoyed the
day all the same.

Neither Jim nor Susan shone in the tournament that
Christmas. They were both unlucky in the draw and were
knocked out in the first round. Susan, however, put up a
very good fight. Once more she got a certain amount of
notice in the press. It did her good. She was even getting
quite a confident air at St. Clair's. When people talked to
her about her tennis, she stopped getting red and
stammering. Everybody said she was good, even the papers.
She herself began to believe it at last.

One day before Easter Nicky and Susan were going up
to practice at the club. They had had their last coaching
some time before and were back again playing games
with each other. Just as they were starting, it started to
pour with rain. Dr. Heath put his nose around his office
door.

"If you two will wait five minutes I'll drive you up. I
might wait and have a look at you. I'd like to see what
that coach has done for you."

They drove up to the club. It was raining cats and
dogs. They ran in laughing and shaking themselves as
Agag did when he had been out in the wet. The secretary
had his door open. He looked out to see who was coming.
He gave them all a friendly smile. Then he seemed to
remember something. He came into the passage.

"Oh, Dr. Heath, I was hoping to see you. As you know,
or perhaps you don't, our coach makes a report on all the
pupils he's had through his hands. If anybody is outstanding, or shows promise, the county sometimes gives
them six lessons. They have decided to do so in this case."

Susan gasped with pleasure. Dr. Heath gave her a
quick smile. The secretary looked at the list in his hand.

167

"Nicolette Heath." He looked at Nicky. "Congratulations, my dear."

The whole family was completely stunned. When as a family you have accepted one person as being supremely good at something, that authorities who ought to know should pick out one of the others, upsets all preconceived ideas. Of course, nobody said very much about it at home because of Susan. Dr. Heath told Mrs. Heath and Pinny. Then he wrote to Grandfather. Susan wrote to Jim:

Dear Jim,

This is only a short extra letter. You know that sometimes the county gives extra coaching at tennis if they think anybody is worthwhile. We heard today that they are giving some to Nicky.

With much love,
Susan

David heard the news from Pinny.

"Nicky's had a little honor done her in tennis, dear. Something we won't talk about. We don't want to upset poor Susan."

As David must not tell anybody, he told Agag.

"Nicky has been chosen for something at tennis. I'm not sure what. I thought you'd like to know."

Nicky told Annie. Annie was dishing up the dinner. She just nodded in an offhand way.

"That's right. Someone's got some sense, I can see. Now run along. No need to think you can hang about in the big top just because someone is giving you lessons for nothing."

Nicky found it a little hard to comport herself decently in the face of her triumph, while at the same time sympa-

168

thizing with Susan. She thought she ought to have had a bit of a party to celebrate, or at least threepence to spend at Mrs. Pettigrew's. Instead, Annie brought in one mince pie and put it in front of Susan.

"That's the last, dear, I've been saving it for you."

Pinny said:

"Susan, dear. There's the duckiest little dress in *Vogue* I want you to look at. I've seen some very cheap material at Lewis's. I thought you'd look sweetly pretty in it."

Nicky felt that she was being neglected.

"Well, if I haven't got a mince pie and nobody's making me a dress, suppose I choose the game for tonight."

Her father looked at her with a twinkle in his eye.

"If I know my Nicky, she's had enough choosing for today."

"Yes, darling," Mrs. Heath said, "we'll play cards. You're fond of that, aren't you, Susan?"

In spite of her triumph, Nicky got into bed feeling cross. There was absolutely nobody to jump about and be pleased with. "Oh, well," she thought, tucking in her back, "if nobody else is pleased, I am." She settled down for the night. "Good night, Nicky, dear. Many congratulations."

Susan heard by Nicky's regular breathing that she was asleep. Suddenly she began to shake. Her teeth chattered. Ever since the secretary had said that at the club, she had been trying not to show anybody that she minded. She had managed to smile and say "Well done" to Nicky, but inside she felt as though she would burst, she was so miserable. All her feelings of not wanting to be looked at, to be just the same as everybody else, came crowding back on her. What a fool she would look now. She had let everybody say how good she was. She had let the girls at school tell her she was marvelous. Why had she never said: "But you ought to see Nicky. She plays better than me"? Perhaps people had always known it. Perhaps they had been laughing at her. How odd that you could wake up in the morning so happy and sure of yourself, and go to sleep the same night with everything gone wrong. She did not mind Nicky being good enough for the county to coach. She only minded that she seemed to have been bolstered up by something that was not true. She sat up and looked into the night. "You're not good at tennis, you conceited fool. Nicky's better than you are. You're not good. People have been telling you lies. You're not good." Suddenly she could not say it anymore. She rolled over on her face on her pillow and sobbed as if she would never stop.

12

Nicky's Career

It was the first day of Easter vacation. Susan asked Jim if he would come to Hampton Court. She was learning about Cardinal Wolsey at school and wanted a good look at where he had lived. Besides, she wanted to talk to Jim somewhere with nobody to bother or interrupt.

On the subway it was too noisy for talking. Besides, they were busy discussing the advertisements. They played the game of marking them all. Ten for full marks. One advertisement they thought so bad they gave it a zero.

After the subway they took a bus to Hampton Court. They got the front seat. Susan looked around. No one was near them to hear what they were talking about.

"You never answered that letter about Nicky."

Jim felt in his pockets for the fares.

"Nothing to say. I don't suppose it means much. I suppose she's good for her age, that's all."

Susan nudged him because the conductor was coming. The conductor said it was a nice day for Hampton Court. They agreed with him. When he had gone, Susan went on with the conversation as if they had not been interrupted.

"She's more than that. I know because of the club. You know how everybody hears things like that. People look at her and point her out. Sometimes they watch her when she's playing. I heard they think she shows more promise than anyone they've ever had."

Jim gave Susan her ticket. He stuck his in a crack under the window.

"Seeing the names on the board, I just don't believe it. If it's true, why didn't we notice it?"

Susan rolled her ticket into a tube.

"She had her wrist at the tournament last summer, then she was in quarantine at Christmas. It's ages since anybody saw her play properly. The person who ought to have known was me. I'm always playing with her. But I suppose if you're trying to do something yourself, you don't notice the other people."

" 'Course you don't," Jim agreed. "Anyway, I dare say you'll be the best in the end."

Susan shook her head.

"Oh, no." She hesitated. "I suppose you'll say 'Sour grapes,' but, honestly, I'm not keen on being good anymore. Just at first I minded, but afterward I suddenly knew I was glad. Tennis is fun if you just enter for doubles and try to get through a round or two of singles, but not when people are expecting you to do something grand. They can do all their expecting about Nicky now."

Jim frowned in a puzzled way.

"I shouldn't think just Nicky being good, if she is, would be enough for Dad. He wants us all to be."

Susan nodded.

"I know. But I think even trying to make us will cost too much. You know, even with all the bits there's never enough in the tennis house for everything. Of course, Grandfather gives us our club subscriptions, and he gave us our first coaching, but he can't go on forever. Think of all the getting about to tournaments, and the rackets and the clothes it will take, if she gets really good."

"Well?" Jim looked at her inquiringly. "What do you want to do?"

"I've been thinking a lot. I'd like Dad and Grandfather to have one of us Wightman Cup Wimbledon standard; they'd be so pleased. I think Nicky could be. Well, let's try and make her. There isn't the money for all of us. I vote it mostly goes on her as the likeliest one."

Jim sighed.

"I can't think of anything more awful than Nicky as a star act."

Susan considered Nicky.

"I don't suppose she'll be awfuller than she often is, anyway. Look! This is where we get off. Now let's pretend Cardinal Wolsey still lives here."

After tea that evening, when Pinny had taken Nicky to the club for her lesson, Dr. Heath came into the living room. Jim and Susan were playing cards. They stopped. Susan thought it was a good moment to talk to him. She explained her idea about Nicky.

"Of course I don't mean," she finished, "that we'd stop working. Only it's quite different just working at something and being a sort of professional at it."

Dr. Heath sat down.

"Professional, indeed! I should hope not." He looked at David, who was lying on his chest, sticking stamps into his album. "What about him? He may have the makings of something good for all we know."

David did not look up from his album.

"Don't trouble about me. I'm fixing my ambitions on my voice. I want to be the man who sings with the band on the radio. I won't have much time for games."

Dr. Heath took his pipe out of his pocket.

"I think you're looking ahead a bit, Susan. I don't know we've any grounds at the moment for thinking Nicky's

173

our only hope. Besides, although the coaches speak well of her, it may be only a flash in the pan."

Susan sat on the arm of her father's chair.

"Well, anyway, she's a flash in the pan. The rest of us aren't that. You know, darling, if you were absolutely honest, you'd own you never have believed much in me."

Her father looked up at her over the match he was holding to the bowl of his pipe.

"You miserable daughter, pinning your poor father down. I thought, and I still think, someday you'll be a very nice player. Quite honestly, I don't think you've the champion's temperament. If it comes to that, all I think about Nicky is that quite suddenly she has come on and is at the moment unusually promising. As for match play, we don't know. We haven't seen her."

Jim took down the tennis house and shook it.

"That's just it. Susan thinks Nicky ought to do a lot of that."

Dr. Heath put his matches back in his pocket.

"What I take it you are trying to tell me is that if it comes to a pinch you'd rather I spread myself on Nicky than try to do you a bit of good all round?"

"That's it, darling." Susan patted his shoulder. "But don't think we're being noble. We're not. It's just, we think it's a worthwhile gamble."

He puffed at his pipe.

"I take it that if you're gambling away your shares out of the tennis house, I can trust all of you to see that if Nicky gets any extra chances she doesn't waste them?"

Jim put the tennis house back on the mantelpiece.

"You bet you can. We'll see the little tyke works."

Susan giggled.

"Poor Nicky! She'll have a dog's life. If she doesn't get to Wimbledon, it won't be our faults."

David caught hold of Agag, who was lying beside him. He stood him up on his hind legs.

"Us two will even give up our singing practice to see she works. Won't we, Agag?"

How Nicky's nose was glued to the grindstone! She would not have minded if it was only her tennis practice she was made to work at; but a good deal of the rest of her time somebody was doing something toward her training.

Susan considered that Nicky ought to know how the great tennis minds of the past had worked. She ransacked the public library for books for her. Nicky, who was no great reader at any time, grew to dread the sight of Susan with books under her arm. She eyed the bundle nervously.

"You've not got another one for me, have you?"

Susan nodded proudly.

"I've managed to get *Lacoste on Tennis.*"

Nicky made a face at the book.

"But I'm still reading Suzanne Lenglen, and I've read Alice Marble."

"When you've finished with Lacoste, I'm getting you Hazel Wightman and Helen Wills, and I expect there are a lot more if I look around."

"Oh, don't look!" Nicky pleaded. "It takes me ages and ages to read even something interesting. But these books I just can't get through."

Nicky would have skimmed the books, but Susan kept her eye on her. Every morning before they got up she gave her a short examination on what she had read the day before.

"What does Kathleen McKane say about smashing and overhead play? What did Betty Nuthall say about footwork? What did Perry say about position on the court?"

Once or twice Nicky refused to answer a question.

175

"I don't know what they said and I don't care. They all say the same things and they all use the same words, and it's miserably dull. I read *The Secret Garden* yesterday, if you want to know. I chose it because nobody plays tennis in it."

"All right," Susan retorted. "If you aren't keen on being good, I don't care. Jim was letting you have an extra racket and making his old one do. I'll write and tell him not to bother."

Something of that sort usually brought Nicky to heel. Not for worlds would she have owned just how keen she was. It was spoiling her reputation for laziness. Without any bullying from any of them she had learned just how hard you had to work to get something even nearly right. She tried to work at the wall when nobody was about. She was not going to have them all looking at each other and saying: "Fancy, do you know I saw Nicky work for over half an hour at just one stroke. You wouldn't have thought she would, would you?" She wanted them to think she was just as lazy as ever, and became good by luck.

It was Jim who invented the part of Nicky's training she hated most. One day in Easter vacation he overheard the coach tell her that she must concentrate more, must not notice what was going on around her. After that he invented games for her. Sometimes it was a general-knowledge paper on things she knew quite well. Sometimes it was a memory test with trays of mixed things. Sometimes tricks, such as picking up peas with knitting needles, or something of the sort. Whatever it was she was going to do, he and Susan did it first. They worked out how long she ought to take. Then they put her at a table with her watch in front of her and told her to begin.

The moment Nicky began the other three began too. But theirs was a different game. They thought out the most ingenious ways of distracting her attention. Once Susan rushed in with a parcel and said: "Look, this has come for me." Jim and David sat down by her. All their backs were to Nicky. Slowly they cut the string and started unwrapping, until finally they all said: "Oh!" Of course Nicky looked up. It was not human nature not to. She was furious she had, when she found it was just an empty box they were staring at.

David thought of dozens of ways of making Agag a distraction. Sometimes he would make him bark. Sometimes he dressed him up. Sometimes he would say: "My goo'ness, look at Agag! He's never done that before." To begin with he nearly always caught Nicky.

Nicky started by never getting any of the things done. She was always looking around and wasting time, and then was made to start all over again until they were worn out. Then quite suddenly one day (it was a day when she was given hundreds of needles to thread) she did them on time. She found she had never heard Jim tell the others they were all going to the movies that night. She had never noticed the roars of laughter when Agag came in dressed as a baby. It was a good many nights after that before she did as well again, but she was improving. When the boys went back to school, Susan carried on with the game and got the grown-ups to help. Nicky nearly always loathed it, because usually she had something else she wanted to do. But she could not get out of it, because Dr. Heath said it was a splendid idea and she was to do it every day. As a matter of fact, it must have been a splendid idea, for by summer vacation she was mostly on time, and if she was not it was because she was stupid at whatever she had been given to do, and not because she lacked concentration. In the end she would not have noticed if the house had fallen down. It was useful. It made her concentration at tennis remarkable. Not from one end of the game to the other did she think of outside things.

Dr. Heath stopped coaching Nicky. He thought she was better left entirely in the coaches' hands. But he made her skip for a quarter of an hour before breakfast every day, and on Saturday afternoons he gave her half an hour's special exercises to make her supple.

Annie, on hearing that "keep your eye on the ball" was important, got Nicky to come to the kitchen every day for ten minutes' juggling. She got to the glorified stage at last of using three balls. She thought, having reached that point, she had done enough, but Annie nipped that in the bud.

"Think it's any fun for me to watch you messin' about with the balls? Well, I'll tell you it's not. But if they're goin' to make a champ of you, Annie's not goin' to be the only one who hasn't done 'er bit. Now then, get on with it, and don't let me hear any more of your nonsense."

As a reward for her efforts she was given a chance of a lot of tournament play that summer. She was to play at Bournemouth, the Pleasure Gardens, Folkestone, the County Junior championship, and the South of England Junior at Eastbourne. Jim and Susan were playing only at Bournemouth and in the County Junior championships.

They were all to stay with Grandfather. Pinny was in even more of a fuss than usual before they started.

"All this match play means more tennis things."

"If you're going to make my things," said Nicky, "for goodness' sake see they don't hang down between the legs. They look simply awful if they do."

Pinny was worried.

"I'll do my best, dear, but there's many a slip, you know, between the cup and the lip."

178

Nicky scowled.

"I'd rather you didn't make them. I'd rather just have two lots ready made. They could wash."

"You need more than two, dear," Pinny explained, "and I've said I'll try."

"And I've said I'd rather you didn't, unless they're right."

Mrs. Heath was writing while this argument went on. She looked up.

"Come here, Nicky." Nicky came over slowly. She could see her mother was cross. "Everybody in this house gives up some of their time to improving your tennis. Now here's Pinny planning to make for you, and all you do is to be rude before you've seen what she's making."

"But you see—" Nicky broke in.

"I see a very spoiled child. Now we don't like punishments, but you must learn you can't behave like that." Mrs. Heath turned to Pinny. "Nicky seems to have clear ideas how she wants her tennis things. Very well, she can cut the pattern herself."

"Oh, I say!" Nicky gasped. "I can't cut a pattern."

Her mother looked at her.

"You should have thought of that before you were rude to Pinny. You will cut a pattern, and it's the only one Pinny will use. And you will wear the dress cut from the pattern at all your tournaments."

Pinny looked horrified. She could not bear the children not to be well turned out.

"Oh, Mrs. Heath—!" she pleaded.

But Mrs. Heath was firm.

"I trust you not to touch the scissors, Pinny. You can give advice if you like, but the cutting Nicky is to do by herself."

It was difficult to know who had the worst afternoon.

For all Pinny's advice, what Nicky cut looked like nothing on earth. Nobody could have worn it. After two and a half hours, Nicky was almost in tears.

"This is over the fortieth I've cut, and I can see it's no good."

"Oh, dear," Pinny sighed, almost in tears herself. "Do try, dear. Remember, if at first you don't succeed, try, try again."

Nicky held up a dreadfully shaped piece of newspaper.

"Do you honestly and truly believe I'll cut a good pattern if I go on trying, Pinny? Do you?"

Pinny struggled between a strict regard for the truth and a wish not to discourage Nicky.

"There's no such word as can't," she said feebly.

Nicky dug the scissors into another piece of paper.

"If there isn't, I expect there will be when I've finished."

At that moment Mrs. Heath came in. She looked at the floor, at Nicky, then at Pinny. Then she burst out laughing.

"I see you've cut plenty of patterns."

The laughter was too much for both Nicky and Pinny. They began to cry.

"They're all awful," Nicky sobbed. "Nobody could ever get them on."

Mrs. Heath picked up a pattern. She looked at it, trying to keep her mouth from turning up at the corners.

"No more they could." She turned to Pinny. "What pattern had you meant to use, Pinny?"

Pinny dabbed her eyes with her handkerchief.

"A nice little McCall."

Mrs. Heath sat down beside Nicky.

"Tomorrow morning we'll ask Pinny to put the McCall over a paper and you shall cut a pattern from it."

Nicky looked up.

"Oh, thank you, Mummy."

"But don't forget," Mrs. Heath added, "it's you that cut it. If it hangs down anywhere, it'll be your fault."

The tennis dresses Pinny made might have been made by a tailor. Nicky looked very nice in them. It was as well she did, for she got a lot of notice that summer. She was small for her age, and with her flaming head she caught the eye. She did nothing very spectacular, but somehow that summer she came definitely on to the junior tennis map. She won no event, although she was a semifinalist at Folkestone and at Eastbourne. But she was news in the way some people suddenly are. No critic described any of the tournaments in which she played without mentioning her. None of the attention given her made her swelled-headed.

"I suppose she couldn't get more proud," Susan said to Jim. "She's always been the proudest person I know."

A sister of Grandfather's was living at Folkestone. Her name was Great-aunt Selina. She lived in a little house overlooking The Leas. She had an old servant, a very aggravating parrot, and a very, very old dog called Pom-Pom, who wheezed a great deal. Great-aunt Selina agreed to put Nicky up for the tournament, provided, as she wrote, "the dear child brings her governess and a brother or sister. One child by herself in a house makes trouble."

It was decided that David should go and, of course, Pinny. Just before they were starting David got a bilious attack from eating too much unripe fruit, so Susan had to go. She was very annoyed, because if she had known she was going she would have entered the tournament. In any case she hated being away in the middle of Jim's vacation.

They got to Folkestone, hot and cross, after a tiresome journey with a lot of changes.

"Lovely, dears," Pinny said as brightly as she could, "to smell the beautiful sea."

"I'd rather smell Grandfather's garden," Nicky argued.

"I like that," said Susan. "We'd none of us be here at all if it wasn't for you."

"Now come along, dears," Pinny said briskly. "Dogs delight to bark and bite, but not two little girls. We must get a porter."

They moved up to the luggage van. It was then the awful thing was discovered. The suitcase was missing.

It was not a good introduction to Great-aunt Selina to arrive with no clothes at all. Pinny bought toothbrushes. They all used Great-aunt Selina's sponge to wash with. They had to sleep in Great-aunt Selina's nightgowns. They were made of linen and were enormous. They had long sleeves and were right up to the neck.

Pinny sent a telegram to Dr. Heath about the luggage. As it happened Dr. Heath was out when the telegram arrived at Grandfather's. In any case, telegraphing him was not the right thing to have done. Pinny should have gone to the stationmaster and the luggage would have been found at once. It would have come either that night, or at least the first thing next morning. As she did not see the stationmaster they woke up in the morning with still no suitcase. At ten o'clock they went around to the Pleasure Gardens. Nicky signed her name on the attendance sheet at the referee's office. She looked at the draw and saw that she was playing against a girl called Coral Dean. She had never heard of her. Then she went to where the list of matches was posted. She had to play Coral at twelve. Luckily she had carried her rackets on the journey, so these at least were with her.

"I must go home for my rackets," she said.

"But, Nicky," Susan exclaimed, "you can't play in those clothes!"

Nicky looked down at the flannel skirt and cotton shirt in which she had traveled.

"Well, what else, then?" she asked. "I haven't any luggage."

"But, Nicky, your shirt's terribly dirty. Anyway it would pull out of your skirt. Then, your pants don't match. You must go and see the secretary. Ask if you could change your time over with somebody else."

"I won't," Nicky objected. "I'll just take off my skirt and play in my shirt and pants."

Pinny grew pink to her ears.

"Oh, no, my dear! You'll do nothing of the sort. Play in your pants, indeed, with everybody watching!"

Nicky looked at her despairingly.

"Why shouldn't I play in pants?"

"Because you can't," said Susan decidedly. "You'll bring shame on all the family. Pinny, tell her she mustn't."

Pinny looked like a flustered hen.

"Certainly you mustn't, Nicky. I forbid it."

Nicky looked at them scornfully.

"I'll start in my skirt, but when I get hot and it gets in my way, I'll take it off. You see if I don't."

Susan looked at Pinny.

"Pinny, we must do something. If the luggage hasn't come we must buy her something to wear."

"Buy, dear!" Pinny was horrified. "Your father gave me a pound for incidental expenses. That has to include the tip to the maid, and teas, and all sorts of things like that. Really, dear, I couldn't break into it. Besides, what could I buy?"

Susan was determined.

"We must ask Great-aunt Selina for money."

183

Nicky giggled.

"She doesn't seem the least the kind of person who would think it mattered what you wore for a game. As a matter of fact, I don't either."

"If you don't ask her, I shall. Come on, Pinny." Susan strode off down the drive of the Pleasure Gardens.

Great-aunt Selina was standing by the window talking to the parrot. Susan came in. She stood in the doorway.

"Pretty Poll," said Great-aunt Selina. "Pretty Poll."

"Pretty Poll," the parrot agreed. Then he gave an ugly shriek.

"Fire, fire, turn her out!"

Great-aunt Selina looked around reproachfully at Susan.

"I thought you were out, dear. You must be more careful how you come into a room. Polly is easily upset."

Susan clasped her hands and hoped she would think of the right thing to say.

"You see, Great-aunt Selina, our luggage is lost and—"

"What, dear?" Great-aunt Selina held her hand to her ear. "Speak up. I'm a little deaf."

"You see"—Susan raised her voice—"Nicky has got to play in her tournament at twelve o'clock."

"Really, dear?" Aunt Selina turned back to her parrot. "Well, I hope it doesn't make you all late for luncheon."

"Yes, but—I mean, I'm sure it won't. But you see she hasn't got her clothes."

"What's the matter with her nose?" Great-aunt Selina looked worried. Then she turned back to the parrot. "Pretty Poll. Pretty Poll."

The parrot fixed an angry eye on Susan.

"You're a thief!" it screamed nastily.

"Really," thought Susan, "if only it were a person I could tell it not to interrupt. It's terribly rude, the things

184

it says. I don't think I really like parrots much." However, she supposed a civil word might keep the bird quiet.

"Pretty Poll," she said soothingly.

The parrot sidled up its perch toward Great-aunt Selina. Its eyes were still on Susan.

"Lazy-bones! Lazy-bones!" it squawked.

Great-aunt Selina heard that all right. It seemed to put an idea into her head. She looked at her wheezy old dog, who was lying in the sunlight.

"If you have nothing to do, dear, you might take Pom-Pom up The Leas. He does enjoy an outing."

"Perhaps after tea. You see, Nicky's match is at twelve, and our luggage has not come."

"You liar!" screamed the parrot.

Susan looked at it with disgust. But she came over to the cage.

"Do be quiet, dear," she said to it. Then she raised her voice to a scream: "What I mean to say, Great-aunt Selina, is, Nicky has not got any clothes to wear to play in, and—"

Great-aunt Selina looked at Susan in surprise.

"I expect she has now, dear. I saw the van from the station drive up while we've been talking."

When Susan came upstairs Nicky was changing.

"I hope you had a nice time with Great-aunt Selina and the parrot," she said. "I nearly came down to tell you that the suitcase had come. But I thought it was a pity to disturb you, you were all being so noisy together."

Susan rummaged in the box for a clean cotton dress. She spoke through her teeth.

"I shouldn't think there's a nastier child living than you, Nicky."

13

The End of the Story

In that next year Nicky became news. The newspapers called her "The Redheaded Pocket Star." Even if she umpired somebody else's match there was nearly always a photograph of her doing it. She did not win anything very spectacular, but she nearly always had a gallery. People who knew anything about tennis were immensely interested in her playing.

At home her family were unremitting in their efforts. Susan was always willing to go up and have a game with her. It was quite impossible for her to miss her wall practice. Even if Susan was not about there was Annie's head coming around the kitchen door.

"Now, then, what's all this sittin' about with a book? Think you've become so good you can miss your practice?"

Or Pinny would come hurrying from her sewing machine.

"Nicky, dear, what are you doing, lolling about like that? Where's your racket? Practice makes perfect, you know."

Nicky often grumbled. She said she wished she had never heard the word *tennis*.

"Work, work, work! You wouldn't think it was a game at all. I think one ought to be able to play without all this slavery."

As a matter of fact, they were all pretty busy with getting on in the world that year. Jim had joined a swimming club. He had taken up diving to add to his swimming. He was very thrilled by it. He had managed, too, to win a cup at the club, which was considered pretty good.

Susan was top of her grade. She was, as usual, working in a class with girls older than herself, so it was considered a bit of a feat. It gave her a definite standing at St. Clair's. As far as tennis was concerned she got more fun out of it now than she ever had. She did not have to worry so much. It became more of a game. She played first string in the school six and would obviously be tennis captain when she was old enough.

Nicky's gradual eminence in the tennis world made very little difference to her position at St. Clair's. She absolutely refused to play for the school, and really you could not blame her. With all the practicing and coaching she had to get through outside it would be a bit too much to expect her to play school tennis. There had been rows at first. Alison Browne and the two tennis captains came and grumbled to Susan. They said that Nicky was unsporting. That for the honor of St. Clair's she ought to play for the school. Alison Browne, of course, talked about the honor of the house. Susan naturally could not say that Nicky cared nothing for the honor of the school, or house, or anything else; that she had not the faintest ambition to see her name on a board; that she liked being a black sheep who never brought a mark to her house. She said instead, as tactfully as she could, that Nicky really did have to put in a lot of practice; it would be too much for her to do any more.

David came on at tennis that year. After his tenth birthday he showed signs of making a nice player. He considered it a very secondary affair, though. His determination to be a entertainer filled his life. It had a most depressing effect on his singing. He rigged himself up something that looked like a microphone and whispered his songs into it. His family complained bitterly.

"It was bad enough your yowling," Jim told him, "but now that you meow and hiss into that box it's downright disgusting."

David was quite unmoved by criticism.

"You won't think it's disgusting when I'm a star on the air."

He discussed his future with Pinny. To her he confided how difficult it was to get support for his wish for an entertainer's life.

"Nobody but myself and Agag," he told her, "really appreciate the idea."

"Well," Pinny said, "I must say, dear, I do like your voice brought full out. I should have liked you to sing in one of the well-known choirs myself. One of those that wears a pretty dress. But, of course, I think your singing beautiful anyway."

When Nicky was thirteen and a half she had her first really big tennis success. She won her match in the semifinal round of the County Junior Championship. All the family came to see her play. It was obvious from the beginning that it was going to be a hard fight. It turned out to be even closer than anyone expected. The match lasted for an hour and thirty-five minutes. As one of the papers said afterward:

"At the end of the match it was not so much a matter of which child had the most strokes, but which had the most willpower."

The family sat in a row. Their eyes were glued on Nicky. If willpower from outside could help, she had it.

Nicky won the first set 6–4. It was a terrific tussle.

188

Every game was carried to advantage points. Her family were exhausted when it was over. Each one of them had played every stroke with her.

"Funny," said David, "when Nicky is on the court she doesn't seem to be ours anymore. She seems to belong just as much to all these other people."

They looked down at her where she stood waiting for the next set to begin. It was true. She did seem a public possession. She was much the younger player. She had a strong personality. Something about her made most of the gallery fond of her. They were willing her to win.

The next set was a real battle. Nicky won the first game. She lost the next. Then she won two in succession, giving her a lead of 3–1. Then her opponent had a spurt. Her service had been a bit faulty in the first set, but now she came on to it and smashed through to win a love game. This gave her confidence. Nicky fought like a tiger, but she lost the set.

"Set all," Dr. Heath whispered to Mrs. Heath. "Now let's see what her fighting spirit's like."

"Oh, dear," David said, "I wish it was over. I'm damp with fuss."

The last set began. Nicky had the first service and won the game. Then her opponent won her service. So it went, ding-dong. 1–love. Game all. 2–1, 2 all. 3–2, 3 all, 4–3. Then Nicky made an extra effort.

She won her opponent's service. The score went 5–3. Nicky began her service. Her opponent, with her back to the wall, fought grandly, but Nicky was outdriving her. She pulled the score to 40–15. Two match points. She served. The ball was returned to her. She got it back, a shot which looked to the gallery untakable, but which by luck rather than anything else her opponent picked up with a backhand half-volley. 40–30. One chance lost, but she still had another. She went behind her baseline to serve. She threw the ball into the air. Then an infuriating thing happened. She served a double fault. Keyed up with excitement, mad at seeing her chance of victory slip, she lost her temper. She flung her racket on the ground. She stamped her foot.

Dr. Heath looked at Mrs. Heath. Mrs. Heath looked at Susan. Susan looked at Jim. Jim looked at David. Nobody needed to say one word. As one person they got up and walked out.

Nicky picked up her racket, feeling an idiot. Deuce. She served again. There was no fault about this one. Over it went. Her opponent had a shot at it, but she drove it into the net. Nicky's advantage. One more point and the match was hers. She served. Rather a feeble one, but still it was over the net. Her opponent sent back a drop shot. Nicky dived at it. It was a glorious finish. A low flat drive across the net. Game, set, and match to Miss Heath.

It was then Nicky realized that her family had gone. She hardly believed it for a minute. How dared they be so mean? To walk out when a member of the family was nearly winning! Just because they were hungry or something. "They never thought, I suppose," she muttered, "that I might be tired after three sets like that. They take the car and leave me to go back by train. I couldn't think anybody could be as unfair as that."

She changed. She managed to smile and thank the people who patted her on the back. Then she went off to the station. On the way home in the train she thought just what she would say to them all. The dirty dogs!

Arrived home, she strutted in at the gate. She ran up the steps. She banged the front door. She marched into the dining room. Everybody was having tea. She stood in the doorway.

"Of all the miserable families, you're the most miserablest. I should have thought anybody would have been enough interested to see whether I won or not to wait five minutes for their tea. Everybody else's families watch their family play." Her voice choked with self-pity. Agag came up to her with wagging tail. He gave her shoe a friendly nip as if to say: "Welcome home."

"Agag," said David severely. "Where's your sense of decency? Come and sit down. You don't want to know a person like that."

Dr. Heath looked at Nicky over his cup. Then he put it down.

"Would you like to hear what I've got to say now, or after you've had your tea?"

"I shouldn't think that anything that any of you've got to say would be much good," said Nicky. "But I'll hear the apology now."

"Apology!" Dr. Heath's voice was very quiet. "I never thought that any child of mine could disgrace us all as you disgraced us this afternoon."

"Me!" gasped Nicky. "Why, I won."

"None of us," her father went on, more quietly than ever, "is in the least interested whether you won or lost. What we are interested in is that you gave one of the worst displays of bad manners that we have ever seen on a court."

Nicky flushed.

"Do you mean because I threw my racket down? Is that what all the fuss is about?"

Dr. Heath nodded.

"You served a double fault, lost your temper, stamped, threw your racket on the grass. The next time I see you lose your temper on the courts, you don't play again. Going on as you are, the day may likely come when you'll be offered hospitality for tournaments. No child of mine is going to become one of those bad-mannered tennis players, giving displays of temper all over the countryside. Making the people who are kind enough to put them up ashamed to have them under the roof. It may even be that someday you may represent your country. After the display we saw this afternoon, I quite hope you won't. Your manners have to be perfect on a tennis court in your own country, but overseas they have to be more than that. I'd rather burn your rackets now than run the risk of your being sufficiently good a player to play for your country and join the ranks of those who, however good their play, have brought disrepute on the British Isles by their manners on the court and off it."

"But—" Nicky interrupted.

"It's all I have to say." Dr. Heath took up his cup again. "The next time I see the slightest hint of bad manners from you on any court, your playing is finished. You understand?"

Nicky nodded. She pulled out her chair and sat down at the table. She looked around. She saw that all the others were a mixture of sorry for her and pleased that she had won. She helped herself to a piece of bread and butter. She took a bite. Then she grinned at her father.

"Miss N. Heath, the pocket star, is very grieved. It won't occur again."

Nicky shot through that summer in a blaze of glory. The mere sight of her brought despair into the hearts of other junior competitors. She picked up so many cups that she had to throw away her musical instruments. The caterpillars had to live on top of the cups. Soon her eleven animals would have to move, she was getting so crushed for space. Susan said that if it was to make room for cups she did not mind lending the top of her bookshelf.

But she was not lending space while eleven animals (that a girl of almost fourteen was too old to have anyway) were using it, not to mention a lot of caterpillars messing up the place. When the animals were all given away, she said, and the caterpillars given up, she would see what she could do.

Although nobody said so, all the family were full of hope that Nicky might do well in the Junior Hard Court Championship that Christmas. It was not to be supposed that she would win it—she was several years younger than any holder had ever been—but she had been a finalist in the the Junior County Championship and she had picked up a lot of awards that summer, and her play had improved. She might manage to get into the semifinal round, which at her age would be remarkable and fill them all with pride.

Nicky herself never said a word about her chances. She never did discuss them. For one thing, none of the family knew about the feeling she got when an audience was with her. A feeling of being lit up inside, able to do anything, of being carried beyond herself.

Nicky was not the only interest in the Junior Hard Court Championship, for they all entered. David startled everybody. He knocked out a boy of about sixteen in the first round. He played abominably in his second match.

"Just as well," he said cheerfully. "Two rounds are quite enough for me with my play coming on." He was singing in a children's play in aid of charity at the end of the holidays.

Susan and Jim startled themselves and everybody else by not being knocked out of the mixed doubles until the semifinal round. They were both a bit embarrassed. They thought they had gone rather beyond themselves and were causing too much attention. They were quite glad when the match was over and they could slink away out of sight. All being redheaded and relations of Nicky's made them, they considered, far too noticeable anyway.

Nicky was only entered for the singles. She was at the top of her form and played her way through steadily. Her family came and watched every match. They pretended not to care, but of course they were bursting with pride really.

After the semifinal round, which Nicky won, Jeffrey Miller came over to Dr. Heath.

"Exciting for you, producing a player like that. Has the makings of the best woman we've bred in this country. Makes me nervous, though, when they're good so young. Afraid it may be just a flash of genius; that she'll outgrow it."

Dr. Heath nodded.

"We're doing what we can to prevent that, by laying a very solid foundation of training."

"Incredibly advanced for something that size. Odd to see a baby use her brains like that. It's going to be a wonderful thing for the country if your Nicolette keeps on as she is now. I'd like to see us with an unbeatable woman." He moved off. "Well, here's to the day when she is old enough for Wimbledon. I'm taking bets on her myself."

After he had gone they all went down to the hall to wait for Nicky. At that moment Pinny came dashing through the club door.

"Oh, Doctor, a telegram! It came over the telephone. I thought it less upsetting to come myself than to ring you up. Your father has had an accident. The dogcart bolted. They say, would you go there at once."

Dr. Heath looked at his watch.

"I don't believe there's a train. I'd better go by car."

194

Mrs. Heath nodded.

"Just stop at the house for a second while we pack some things."

He looked down at her, surprised.

"We? You don't want to come?"

She looked at him exactly as she looked at the children when they talked nonsense.

"Of course I'm coming." She turned to Susan. "Susan, dear, find Nicky and tell her we've had to go. I expect she'd like all of you to wait and walk back with her."

Nicky, with her hair sticking to her forehead, had just had a shower. She was beginning to change. Susan told her what had happened.

"Goodness!" Nicky's eyes filled with tears. "How awful! Do you suppose he's bad? I mean, is he going to die?"

"I don't expect so," Susan said as firmly as she could, although she felt the gravest misgivings inside. "Dad will telephone tonight, I expect, and let us know."

Nicky gave her a push.

"Well, go on! See that you make him promise to telephone. None of you wait for me. I'm awfully hot. I don't want to hurry. I'm going to have tea here. I'll come home presently."

Nicky finished changing. She had tea with her late opponent. Then she decided to walk home. She thought about Grandfather. She did hope he was not badly hurt. It would be the most miserable thing if he was. She turned gloomily into their street. Then she stopped. Around the corner came a man pushing a cart. At the end of the cart were balloons and those paper things that spin around. As he came nearer she could see that on the cart were jam jars, some old clothes, and three umbrellas. It was at the umbrellas that Nicky stared. She hurried up the street toward the cart. She stood in front of the man.

"Do you remember me?"

"No, miss." The man stopped his cart. "Can't say as I do."

"I remember you very well," Nicky said sternly, "and a very nasty memory it is. You are the man who gave me one and a penny for all the umbrellas in the umbrella stand. Four there were. They were worth an awful lot really."

"Were they, now?" The man scratched his head. "Four umbrellas, did you say? When was this, miss? I can't bring it to mind."

"Years and years ago," said Nicky. "When I was little."

"Oh!" The man shook his head. "Years and years ago. Never 'arbor a grievance. That's what I said to the copper what come poking his nose around my shop. 'What are you lookin' for?' I said. 'There's nothing here what shouldn't be.' 'If there isn't,' he says to me, 'it'll be about the first time.' So I holds up a finger at him. 'Young man,' I says, 'that's 'arboring a grievance, that is.' "

Nicky looked at him in disgust.

"You'd have harbored a grievance if you'd been me. Do you know that I had no birthday presents from my father and mother for two years? And no Christmas presents for two years? Instead, they kept putting an umbrella back in the stand."

"Did they now?" The man made shocked clicking noises. "Unfeeling, that was."

"And what was more," said Nicky, "it was in a good cause I wanted the money. It was for the tennis house."

"The tennis house?" He looked puzzled.

Nicky lolled against the cart.

"Oh, you wouldn't know about that. It's a house made of silver. It's about this high." She held her hands apart to give a suggestion of the height. "It has a chimney that

196

pulls down, and under it is a slot. We keep the house on the living-room mantelpiece and everybody puts everything into it they can. It's to pay for the extra things for tennis. That's why it's called the tennis house. I owed it one and a penny when I saw you last, and you were mean enough only to give me that for four umbrellas."

The man gave her a warning look.

"Now, now, no 'arboring a grievance. That's what we said. Have you got anything you want to sell today? I might give you a good price."

"If I had, I wouldn't sell it to you. If you're cheated once, you expect to be cheated again. As a matter of fact I'm much too worried today to think of money. We've just had a telegram. Grandfather's had an accident. Mother and Father have gone off in the car to see how he is."

The man put on a grave expression as of somebody going to a funeral.

"That's bad. I'm sorry to hear that. Maybe a little ready money would take your mind off your troubles."

"It wouldn't," said Nicky. "Besides, as a matter of fact the tennis house is very full just now. There's nearly six pounds in it. That's because of our Christmas money, and some jumpers Pinny knitted, and some money Daddy had from a grateful patient as a Christmas present."

"Six pounds!" The man looked impressed. "My, that's a lot of money! Well, I must be toddling." He picked up his cart and pushed it slowly up the road.

Nicky was cold from standing still. She ran the rest of the way home. The umbrella man stopped and put down his cart. He turned to look after Nicky. He watched her open the gate of the house and disappear. Then he seemed to change his mind. He turned his cart around. He pushed it back the way he had come. He stopped a moment outside the Heath's house. His face was thoughtful.

The telephone call about Grandfather came through while they were having supper. Annie was feeling very sorry for them all and had made them an especially nice supper, but none of them could eat it. The house felt miserable without their father and mother, and every time they thought about Grandfather they got a sinking feeling inside. When the telephone bell rang, they all got up and ran to answer it. It was Jim who got there first. He picked up the receiver. The others stood around and listened.

"Hello, old man!" Dr. Heath sounded quite cheerful. "Things are not so bad. Grandfather has broken his leg. We've got him into a nursing home at Salisbury. He's just been X-rayed. It's not too bad a break. The first thing he asked about was how Nicky was doing in the match. He wants us to get back in time to see her play tomorrow. I can't say for certain if we shall be able to do that. I must wait about to see if there are likely to be complications from the shock, but tell Nicky we shall do our best to be there."

"Do you mean," Jim asked, "that honestly Grandfather is not really bad?"

"Honestly. It's a straightforward break. There's no reason on earth why he shouldn't be completely himself in a couple of months."

The three-minute time signal clicked across their conversation.

"Good-bye, old man."

"Good-bye, Dad."

They were all so glad to know that Grandfather had only broken his leg and was not going to die that they changed their minds about eating supper. They ate up all there was, and then got Annie to give them some cold plum pudding as well. After that they settled down to a game. They played until nine. Pinny came in every two minutes to say it was a disgrace and David ought to be in bed, but he said, if she held the cards that he did, she wouldn't even think of bed. However, at nine he had to go, and a quarter of an hour later Nicky went too. Then at half-past Jim and Susan decided they were sleepy. By eleven everybody in the house was asleep.

It was two o'clock in the morning when Jim heard the noise. He and David slept over the living room. Some sound had waked him. He sat up. Whatever could it be? Was it Agag in the flower room? Had he barked? Then suddenly he grew stiff. There was the noise again. It was a window opening. Very quietly he got out of bed. He pulled on his dressing gown. Somebody was certainly opening a window downstairs. He tied the cord round his waist and in doing so the tassel flicked across David's face in the other bed. David grumbled. He moved. In a second Jim was leaning over him. He put his hand over his mouth.

"Shh! Don't make a sound!"

David sat up.

"What is it?" he asked sleepily.

"Somebody is in the house," Jim explained. "They are opening the living-room window. I'm going down to see who it is."

"Oh, goo'ness!" David got out of bed. At once he put on the manner he thought a detective should wear. He slithered into his dressing gown so quietly that even Jim hardly heard him. "Ought we to disguise ourselves?" he whispered.

"Don't be a fool," said Jim. "You had much better stay up here. No good a whole lot of us getting mixed up in it."

David crept over toward the door.

"Don't be a fool yourself," he retorted. "If there's burglars, do you think I'm going to miss them?" He listened. "I do hope Agag hasn't been drugged. I can't think why he isn't barking."

Jim did not bother to answer. He began very cautiously turning the handle of the door.

It's extraordinary how stairs that never have a sound in them in the daytime creak at night. Every stair made its moan. Jim and David slipped down into the hall.

They walked on tiptoe to the living room. They listened. At first they heard nothing. Then they heard a slight noise. It was as though someone were moving about inside and had run into a chair. Then there was a chink.

David looked at Jim.

"That's the tennis house."

Jim leaned down to him.

"That means whoever it is, is over by the mantelpiece. Do you think, if I open the door, you could slip in first and turn on the lights? I want to make straight at him."

"Couldn't you turn on the lights and me do the tackling?" David suggested.

Jim thought this idea not worth answering. He laid his hand on the door handle. He turned it softly.

"Ready?"

He flung the door open. David was on the lights in a second. For one moment they were blinded. Then they saw a man, in a mask and gloves, running for the window. In a moment Jim was after him. He dived at him and caught him by the knees. The man crashed to the floor on his face. The tennis house, which was in his hand, rolled away under a chair. David picked up a cushion off the sofa. He put it firmly on the man's head and sat down on it.

There is nothing more difficult to do than to get up

when somebody is sitting on your head, especially when you are half suffocated by a cushion. Jim did not think it was an artistic way to treat a burglar, but it was a good idea, so he sat down on the small of the man's back. It was not easy for either Jim or David to remain seated, as the man thrashed about cursing and trying to free himself.

"My goo'ness!" said David, tossing from side to side. "What do we do now? Do we sit here all night?"

"I don't think we can," Jim gasped.

He was quite right, for at that moment the man reared up and threw David off him, then, the moment his head was free, he rolled over and seized hold of Jim. David looked around for the best thing with which to help. At Eastbourne he was being taught how to box. But all he had learned at boxing was no good to him now, because the part of the man that he could reach as he and Jim rolled over and over was below the belt, and therefore outside his boxing instructions. Instead, he threw himself at one of the legs and held on to it with his teeth. The man let out a squawk, but David clung on.

At that moment the door opened and Pinny came in. If Jim and David had not been so busy, they would have laughed. Pinny had on a red flannel dressing gown; her hair was done up in curlers, around her shoulders was a pink woolly shawl. She had taken out her false teeth for the night, so she did not speak very well.

"Oh, dear," she said in a muffled way, "don't be rough, boys."

"Come here, Pinny," Jim called out, for at that moment he was on the upper side. "Come and sit down on him."

"Sit on him!" Pinny looked shocked. "Surely not, dear. I don't think it would be nice."

"Come on!" Jim called desperately. "He's a burglar."

"A burglar!" Pinny looked at what she could see of the

201

man in disgust. Then sat down on the nearest bit of him, which happened to be his knees. David took advantage of this and let go of the ankle and sat down on the feet. Jim, panting but triumphant, sat on the shoulders. Pinny looked cautiously down at her bit of the man.

"Are you sure he's a burglar, Jim, dear? Oughtn't we to ask him?"

Before Jim could answer the door opened, and Annie raced in. She had not even bothered to put on a dressing gown. She had nothing on but a flannel nightgown. In one hand she carried a poker, in the other a saucepan lid. She needed no advice as to what to do. She sat down at once on the only bit of the burglar left, which was his head. She raised her poker in the air.

"I'll knock him out!" she said. "The dirty gangster!"

Jim caught her arm.

"Don't do that, you might kill him. One of us must call the police."

The word *police* stirred the burglar to further efforts. He heaved all over, but it is difficult to shake off four people who are sitting on you at once.

Jim looked at them all.

"The thing is, which of us can best be spared to telephone?" David was valuable on the feet and not very good with the telephone. Pinny would almost certainly call the fire brigade by mistake. He could not be spared. Annie must go. "Annie," he said, "you go. Leave the front door open and tell them to come straight in. And tell them to be quick about it."

While Annie was telephoning, the burglar made noises. He was obviously appealing to be let go. But it was difficult to hear what he said, because his nose and mouth were pressed into the carpet and Jim was sitting on his

202

neck. After a few moments Annie came back. With her came Susan.

"I heard the noise," said Susan, "but I couldn't come before because when I moved, Nicky turned over in bed. I was afraid she would wake up."

"She hasn't waked, has she?" Jim asked anxiously. "You're sure?"

"Absolutely." Susan nodded. "When I got outside I listened, and there wasn't a sound."

David gave a thankful sigh.

"Well, that's a good thing. It would be most maddening if Nicky was upset before her match after all the trouble we've taken."

It seemed no time after that before the room was full of policemen. They had all hoped for a lot of cross-examining, but there was not much. The man was put into handcuffs and his mask taken off, and he was walked away. The policeman said they would be back in the morning. After the front door was shut they all felt a bit flat. It was Annie who had the bright idea.

"If you all go back in the living room, I'll make you a nice cup of cocoa. But mind you're quiet. We don't want Nicky disturbed. We'll tell her about it in the morning."

Just as the cocoa arrived David remembered Agag. He got up, quite pale with fright.

"I believe Agag has been poisoned, otherwise he would have been bound to bark, being the watchdog he is."

As quietly as possible they ran to the flower room and turned on the light. The rug was right over Agag's basket. The shape of his body showed, but no sign of his breathing. Gently Jim uncovered him. He lay stiff and rigid, without a sign of life. David leaned down and patted him.

"Agag," he whispered desperately. "Agag, old man."

Agag looked up. He opened first his brown eye, then his blue. He stared at them all in surprise, as much as to say: "What an hour to wake up a tired dog!" Then he rolled over and went to sleep again. Jim tucked him in. David looked at the basket with a puzzled air.

"It's absolutely certain," he said, "with a rug over your head, you can't hear anything. If Agag had heard one single sound, he would have bitten that man to the bone."

"I hope not, dear," said Pinny. "Such a gentle little dog. Come and drink your cocoa before it's cold."

The other three, Pinny, and Annie came to watch Nicky's great match. It was a very tense afternoon, because the other finalist had got as far as that for the last three years, and always been beaten. Next year she would be too old to play. She was out to win.

The game began rather dully, both the players a bit tentative. Nicky was the first to get on to her game. She found a good length for her drives and then carried on the attack by her volleying length. Then her opponent picked up. She got in some very nasty drop shots which just nipped over the net and were unreturnable. They leveled up at four games all. Then, when the score was 40–30 in the ninth game, with Nicky in the lead, she got in a very remarkable half-length backhand drive. This brought her rounds of applause from the gallery. Applause always stimulated Nicky. It did this time. She smashed her way through the next game, with the loss of only a point, and won the first set.

Up until that moment she had been so intent on the game that she had never thought of her family. In the pause before the next set started, she looked up to see if by chance her father and mother had arrived. It was then she discovered that not only had they not arrived, but her whole family had walked out on her. For a moment Nicky was so stunned, her breath was taken away. Here she was playing a most important championship and they had all gone. Then a cold feeling seized her inside. Had she, while she was busy on the game, shown temper or bad manners? She was sure she had not. They had just imagined it. Very well, then, the dirty dogs, she would show the lot of them she could win without them.

The last set Nicky ceased to be herself at all. She felt just a brain and a racket. She dashed about the court; she smashed here, volleyed there. Her opponent tried to strengthen her defense by an increase of pace, but Nicky, in the mood she was in, was too good for her. With the loss of only three games to that set she won the championship.

Nicky succeeded in smiling and being grateful for all the congratulations she received, but it was acting. Inside she was blazing with temper. She went home with her eyes glinting and her lips set. The car was outside the door. Her father and mother must have come home. Well, they would hear how she was treated. Inside the hall her mother's suitcase was standing. The living-room door was open. Everybody was there, including Annie and Pinny. They were all talking at once. They still had on their hats and coats. Nicky burst in.

"I suppose none of you care that Miss N. Heath, at the age of fourteen, has won a championship which nobody of her age has ever won before?"

Jim had his back to her. He turned around.

"You may be good at tennis, Nicky, but, my goodness, you're a fool at everything else. We left the club because we had a message to go to the police court, about that burglar."

"Didn't you guess who he was, Nicky?" Susan broke in.

"He said you told him where the tennis house was and that it had six pounds in it."

"We only wondered you didn't open the front door for him too," said David.

"Do you mean to say it was my umbrella man?" Nicky asked. They all nodded. "The loathly worm! I wouldn't have thought there could be so nasty a man in the world."

The telephone rang. Dr. Heath went to answer it.

"We called the club, dear," said Mrs. Heath, "and heard you won your match. It's splendid."

Annie moved to the door. "If you'll go and take your things off, all of you, tea will be coming over in two shakes."

Dr. Heath came back.

"Was it Grandfather?" Susan asked anxiously.

He shook his head. He looked at Nicky with a funny smile.

"It was Jeffrey Miller, to congratulate you, Nicky. He said we must be careful not to let you get spoiled."

"Spoiled!" Nicky's tone was most expressive. "A fat lot of spoiling I get!"

"Don't be such an idiot," said Jim. "You don't need telling we're all awfully pleased. You don't care a bit if we're watching or not. You know that."

"Aren't you clever?" Nicky made a face at him. "The odd thing is, I do care. So there!"

Annie poked her head around the door.

"Will you all go and take your things off? Tea's just coming over." She looked around. "There's meringues. The right food for a champ."

"Meringues! For all of us?" asked David anxiously. "Or just Nicky?"

Annie snorted.

"All of you, of course." She looked at Agag, who was playing with one of Nicky's tennis shoes. "Even him. There's no favorites in this house."

DANCING

If dancing holds a special magic for you, don't miss these charming stories. Set in England before you were born, they follow the amusing adventures of some *very* talented children.

___BALLET SHOES
    41508-X-54 ....$3.25

___DANCING SHOES
    42289-2-57 ....$2.95

___MOVIE SHOES
    45815-3-46 ....$3.25

___SKATING SHOES
    47731-X-35 ....$2.75

___THEATRE SHOES
    48791-9-06 ....$2.95

___TRAVELING SHOES
    48732-3-32 ....$2.95
    Not available in Canada.

by Noel Streatfeild

At your local bookstore or use this handy coupon for ordering:

Dell DELL READERS SERVICE—DEPT. B471A
P.O. BOX 1000, PINE BROOK, N.J. 07058

Please send me the above title(s). I am enclosing $_____ (please add 75¢ per copy to cover postage and handling.) Send check or money order—no cash or CODs. Please allow 3-4 weeks for shipment.

Ms./Mrs./Mr._____

Address_____

City/State_____ Zip_____